DANA STABENOW

DEATH

OF AN

EYE

HEAD
of ZEUS

First published in the UK in 2018 by Head of Zeus Ltd

9 7 5 3 1 2 4 6 8

A catalogue record for this book is available from
the British Library.

ISBN (HB): 9781788549196
ISBN (XTPB): 9781788549202
ISBN (E): 9781788549189

Typeset by Adrian McLaughlin

Printed and bound in Great Britain by
CPI Group (UK) Ltd, Croydon CR0 4YY

Head of Zeus Ltd
5–8 Hardwick Street
London EC1R 4RG
WWW.HEADOFZEUS.COM

DEATH OF AN EYE

DANA STABENOW, born in Alaska and raised on a 75-foot fish tender, is the author of the award-winning, bestselling Kate Shugak series. The first book in the series, *A Cold Day for Murder*, received an Edgar Award from the Mystery Writers of America. Contact Dana via her website: www.stabenow.com

This one is for Scott Gere
who helped me build a hybrid publishing
business model that lets me write what
I want to, at least some of the time.

This book is the result.

Thanks, Scott.

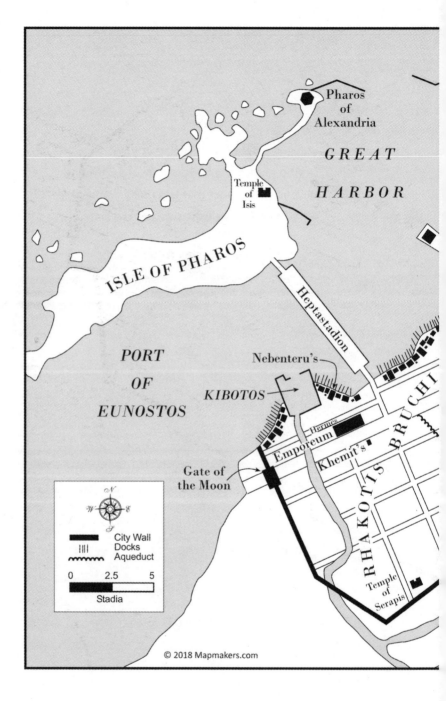

Pharos
of
Alexandria

GREAT

HARBOR

Temple
of
Isis

ISLE OF PHAROS

Heptastadion

PORT

OF

EUNOSTOS

Nebenteru's

KIBOTOS

Hermes
Emporeum

Khemit's

Gate of
the Moon

RHAKOTIS

BRUCHI

Temple
of
Serapis

N
W · E
S

City Wall
Docks
Aqueduct

0   2.5   5

Stadia

© 2018 Mapmakers.com

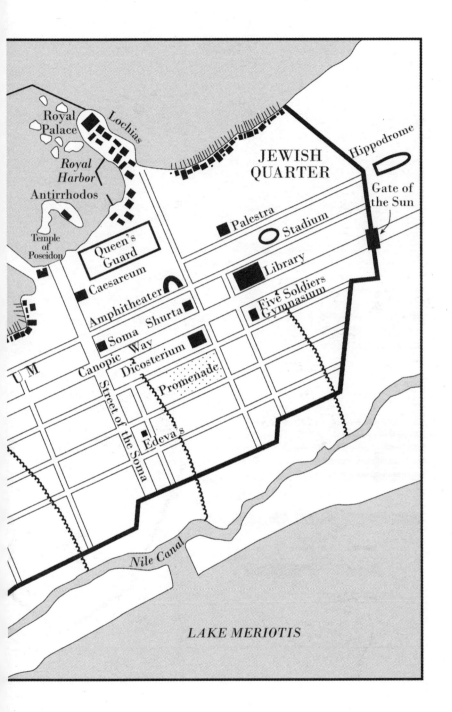

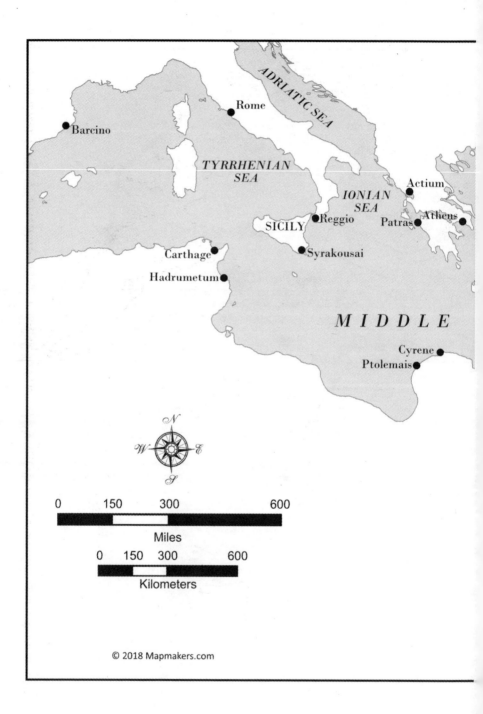

© 2018 Mapmakers.com

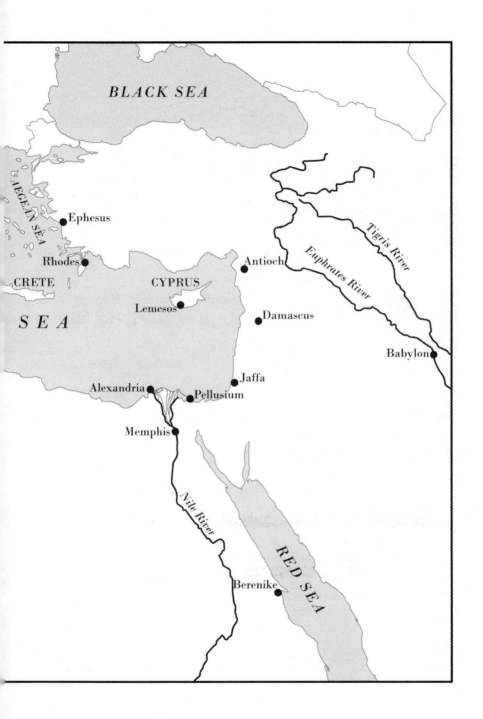

CAST OF CHARACTERS

Amenemhet	Nomarch of the Crocodile, friend of Nebenteru
Apollodorus	Partner in the Five Soldiers, Cleopatra's personal guard
Aristander	Head of the Shurta, the local police
Arsinoë	Daughter of Ptolemy XII Auletes, Cleopatra's sister
Atet	Employee of Khemit, wife of Ineni
Bolgios	the Gaul Crew on *Thalassa*
Cassius	Gaius Cassius Longinus, Senator of Rome, father of Naevius and Petronius
Castus	Partner in the Five Soldiers
Charmion	The queen's personal servant
Cleopatra VII	Queen of Alexandria and Upper and Lower Egypt
Crixus	Partner in the Five Soldiers
Cordros	Gem merchant, friend of Uncle Neb
Cotta, aka Aurelius Cotta	Caesar's cousin and trusted aide
Debu the Egyptian	First mate on *Thalassa*
Dubnorix	Partner in the Five Soldiers
Edeva	Taverna proprietor, daughter of Old Pert
Gelo	Paulinos' second-in-command

Gnaeus Lentulus	Owner of a ludus in Capua
Harmon	Master of Laogonus' workshop
Hunefer	Nomarch of Marimda, follower of Ptolemy XIV, Tetisheri's former husband
Ineni	a prosperous flax farmer
Ipwet	Hunefer's mother
Isidorus	Partner in the Five Soldiers
Julius Caesar	General, Senator and Consul of Rome
Keren	Student of medicine
Khemit	A weaver and the Queen's Eye
Kiya	Wife of Amenemhet
Laogonus	Owner and captain of *Thalassa*
Leon the Iberian	Crew on *Thalassa*
Linos the Eunuch	Political advisor to Ptolemy XIV
Naevius	Son of Gaius Cassius Longinus
Nebenteru	Uncle Neb, Tetisheri's uncle and partner in Nebenteru's Luxury Goods
Nebet	Hunefer's cook
Nenwef	Friend of Hunefer
Nike	Hunefer's former slave
Old Pert the Pict	Crew on *Thalassa*
Paulinos Longinus	Shipping agent, father of Paulina
Petronius	Son of Gaius Cassius Longinus
Philo	Advisor to Ptolemy XIV
Polykarpus	Advisor to Ptolemy XIV, former advisor to Arsinoë
Ptolemy XII Auletes	Cleopatra's father
Ptolemy XIV Theos	Cleopatra's brother and co-ruler
Ptolemy XV Caesarion	Son of Caesar and Cleopatra
Sosigenes	The queen's chief counselor
Tarset	Chief assistant to Khemit the weaver
Tetisheri	Friend and confidante of Cleopatra, partner in Nebenteru's Luxury Goods
Thales	Egyptian general, advisor to Ptolemy XIV
Zoe	Wife of General Thales
Zotikos	The queen's physician

Honestly, I think historians are all mad.

—JOSEPHINE TEY

PRÓLOGOS

*in the Sixth Year of the reign of Cleopatra VII
in Mesore, the Fourth Month of Shemu, the season of
harvest on the Ninth Day of the Second Week
at the Nineteenth Hour...*

Sefkhet, as she was called by the Egyptians, Selene by the Greeks, cast her pale-faced glory upon the storied city on the southeastern edge of the Middle Sea, turning columned palaces and marbled streets into a city of ghosts, luminous, shifting, dreamlike, a place of legends that had only gained in renown in the three hundred years since its founding.

To the north, the Middle Sea was a continuous ripple of gilt, Lake Mareotis a shadowed mirror to the south, the Nile a slender silver ribbon to the east, all of them bathed in the glow of her care. Nothing escaped her eye. The woman in labor all night in her home in the Egyptian Quarter near the Western Gate had finally given birth to a fine, lusty son and both were now deep asleep. In a house in the Royal Quarter events were occurring that saddened her, but things like that were best left to the judgement of Hathor and she moved on. The queen slept in the Royal Palace next to the man she had chosen as her consort, and was ripe with his child. Sefkhet was not an admirer, as he was a worshipper of alien gods, but the queen was strong and intelligent and fit to rule a land as diverse as this one and thus far Sefkhet had reserved judgement.

The light of Pharos flashed far out to sea, alerting mariners due to arrive the following morning. Boats that had already made port bobbed at anchor and at the docks of the Port of Eunostos. In Rhakotis a seaman stirred next to the woman he had hired for the evening, dreaming of his wife far to the north.

Alexandria slept, beautiful and silent and still, beneath Sefkhet's watchful eye, and she was content.

And yet... no, not everyone slept. There were those abroad on the queen's business, necessary business, and dangerous, too. Far below on one of those marbled streets sandals whispered over cool stone. A slender form wrapped in a dark cloak from head to ankle slipped from shadow to shadow, disturbing the air no more than a zephyr wafting ashore. The two men she followed were less cautious, or perhaps less practiced in moving silently.

Yes, there were others out on business of their own as well, and less savory business to be sure. Sefkhet was annoyed at this unseemly and unnatural disturbance and was half inclined to intervene, but she yearned toward the horizon and her own rest. Besides, there was her brother Ra rising from his own sleep behind her, now only a suggestion of radiant light on the eastern horizon but soon to be a blinding, golden glow. She prepared to lay herself to rest.

The momentary dark between moonset and sunrise was merciful in that the woman moving between shadows in the street below never saw the upraised arm or the weapon in the clenched fist. So concentrated on the words of the two men she was following, so intent on getting close enough to overhear their low-voiced conversation, she did not hear the scuff of different sandals behind her, sandals worn by an unsuspected third conspirator. She knew only a sudden shock, and then an immediate sensation of falling into a darkness even deeper than that of the night. She never felt the hard, cool marble beneath her cheek, or smelled the coppery scent of her own blood, or saw the dark pool spreading from beneath her head, or heard the frantic scurry of hurrying feet fading into the distance.

A round, flat blue stone slipped from her bodice and fell to the marble tile with a distant click, suspended crookedly from the chain around her neck. When Ra in all his glory mounted the eastern horizon a moment later, the nacre inlay of the stone's eye gleamed in the light of a new day.

And the dead woman's ka rose from her body and drifted south on the wind.

1

*on the morning of the Tenth Day of the Second Week
at the Fifth Hour...*

"Sheri! Where are you, girl? Sheri!"

"Uncle Neb! You're back!" A slim woman materialized from the depths of the house. She ran forward to throw her arms around the speaker. He raised her off her feet and squeezed her so hard it caused a breathless protest.

Nebenteru the Trader (Imports and Exports, Dealing Exclusively in Luxury Goods Fine and Rare, Prices Available Upon Request, Commissions Negotiated) was a man made to chuckle and he did so now, all two bellies and three chins shaking as he set her down again. "Wait till you see the treasures I have brought downriver!" He spread his arms wide and raised his face to the sky, as if imploring Hathor herself to witness his words. "The merchants of Alexandria will weep with envy and we shall be rich beyond dreams of avarice!"

Tetisheri regarded him with affection. His hair was black and his skin was dark, in part from their common Theban ancestors and in part from long days spent shepherding shipments up and down the Nile and across the Middle Sea. His eyes were large and dark brown and thickly lashed and drew up slightly at the outer corners. Like Tetisheri's own but that hers were a clear blue, a blue as deep and dark as the Middle Sea itself.

As dark as he, she was taller by a hand and slender where he was stout, she was simply dressed in a slim tunic of white Egyptian cotton, her only ornament a tiny chalcedony pendant in the shape of an exquisitely carved black cat hanging from a silken cord around her neck. By contrast Uncle Neb was a bit of a dandy. His tunic and trousers were made of the finest linen from the looms of the city's most talented weavers, the sash that bound them a marvel of red and gold thread. His hair was close-cropped and always neatly trimmed, and his beard was drawn into a point off his chin and that point adorned with a large, tear-shaped pearl that trembled violently as he talked and laughed. It trembled now as he caught her shoulders in his hands and looked her over. "All is well with you then, Tetisheri?"

She smiled down at him, hands raising to clasp his. "All is well, Uncle Neb."

"Breaking any hearts?"

She made a face. "Not lately." Not since her disaster of a marriage had ended two years before, and not ever again if she had anything to say about it.

He raised an eyebrow but forbore to comment. "And the business? Sales are booming?" They turned as one toward the back of the house, her arm settling around his shoulders and his about her waist.

"The business goes well, Uncle, although there has been more trading than selling, and what we sell is bought mostly with denarii. You've heard the news? That Caesar is leaving soon?"

He nodded. "I passed him and the queen coming upriver as I was coming down."

"I saw them leave. It was quite the procession."

"Difficult to believe the royal barge didn't sink beneath the weight of the statuary she loaded on board."

"Living and dead," Tetisheri said, and they both laughed. "I hope Caesar was properly impressed."

"As he was meant to be."

"As he was meant to be. But my point is, Uncle, is that with Caesar and his men leaving soon, we might like to look at the inventory. As long as there is one Roman left in all of Egypt we can never stock enough olive oil, but there might be less call for garum."

"Caesar is not the man to leave a prize as rich as Egypt unguarded, Sheri." Uncle Neb shook his head. "Nor is he so unwise or so unambitious as to leave a puppet behind with no minder, lest she cut her strings."

"The queen is no puppet, Uncle."

"You've known her longest and best," he said agreeably, and left the *but* unsaid. "Regardless, I venture to say that there will be Romans enough left behind when Caesar goes to maintain a healthy profit on any amount of garum we care to stock."

Tetisheri's frown deepened. "Very likely you're right." A young woman entered the room. "Yes, Keren?"

"You have a caller. He waits in the atrium."

"Thank you." She kissed Neb's cheek. "Go gloat over your treasures. I'll be with you in a moment."

"Well met, Keren!" Neb said. "You won't believe what I found for you!"

"I won't?"

"Indeed, in a little shop in the souk in Berenike. An enormous collection of healing herbs such as would have wrung your heart at the very sight."

"You went all the way to Berenike?"

He waved a negligent hand. "An easy diversion from Syrene, and well worth the journey. The trade goods on the docks of Berenike, Keren, you should have seen the variety, from as far away as Punt and Sinae! It was marvelous to behold."

"Were there any seeds with these faraway herbs that you found, Uncle?"

He grinned at her. "Seeds for all of them."

"Uncle! And did you bring some of each back for me, too?"

He pretended offense. "What do you take me for, child? Of course I did."

Their voices faded as Tetisheri made her way to the

atrium, a large, square room open to the sky. A fountain made of simple white marble tiers shaped into staggered rounds trickled pleasantly from one level to the next and finally into a small pool beneath. Citrus and pomegranate trees flourished in every corner.

Her pace slowed when she saw who was waiting for her.

He was looking into the pool, a contemplative expression on his face, and he did not hear her at first so that she was able to study him for a few moments. He was tall with a trim figure that gave the impression of motion even when at rest. His brown tunic was made from a rough weave and girdled by a wide belt bearing a gladius in a boiled leather sheath. Wide guards stamped with double-headed eagles bound both wrists, their leather well oiled and supple from use. Old scars gleamed whitely against his skin, across an eyebrow, a cheekbone, his jaw, both arms, slanted deeply across a calf, a history of service under arms, although he was anything but the grizzled old soldier. His hair was fair and thick, cut close to his head. He could have been any age from twenty to forty.

He looked up. His eyes were the color of olivine, pale and clear and of a quality that one instinctively felt pierced directly to the heart of any matter, suffering no ambiguity, equivocation, or outright lie.

"Tetisheri," he said. His voice was deep and steady.

"Apollodorus."

"She wants to see you."

She cast a look behind her, ready with excuses of a newly

returned uncle and a massive intake in inventory to be accounted.

"Immediately."

Her lips tightened briefly, and then relaxed. "I'll get my cloak."

2

on the morning of the Tenth Day of the Second Week
at the Sixth Hour...

Nebenteru's Luxury Goods boasted a prime central location on Hermes Street, which followed the docks lining the Port of Eunostos, which meant they could avoid the crowds and commotion of the Canopic Way by walking along the edge of the harbor. The manmade Port of Kibotos was behind them, Kibotos being the port of entry for the canal leading to the Nile, where all upriver traffic stopped to be checked by Customs for duty and by the Shurta for contraband. Coming up on their left was the Heptastadion, the causeway connecting the city with the Isle of Pharos. The island's eastern end was dominated by the lighthouse, so tall and the flame of its light made so bright by reflecting mirrors that it could be seen from ships as far as ten leagues at sea. It could be seen from everywhere in Alexandria, too, and was the lodestone by which its citizens navigated about their city.

It was a day as beautiful as were most days in Alexandria, a city benefiting from an idyllic location between the stifling heat of the interior deserts and the cool, onshore winds of the Middle Sea. Sunlight skipped across the ripples of the water, against which the Pharos stood tall and proud. The air smelled of salt. Gulls soared and dived and called raucously to one another, second in volume only to the low, continuous roar of the streets of Alexandria by day. A fisherman was selling his early morning catch off the stern of his boat and was surrounded by a gaggle of slaves and housewives bargaining furiously at the tops of their voices for only the best shrimp and squid and fish for that evening's dinner. Stalls lining both sides of the street featured onions, leeks, and garlic, lentils, beans and spices, dates, figs, plums, pomegranates, melons and more. The latest in food and fashion from Rome, Athens, and Byzantium was hawked from the decks of larger ships, and the wealth of brightly colored fruits and fabrics was enough to blind the eye.

The spaces between the vendors were, as always, well seeded with individuals hoping to gather a few coins in their bowls with magic tricks, juggling, and acrobatics. There were many musicians with varying degrees of talent, like the young Greek man who tootled mournfully on a flute, in accompaniment with another young Greek who sang a song of losing his mother, his job, and his dog all on the same day. They were very attractive young men, which accounted for the circle of adoring young women surrounding them. Here a man aged either by nature or by craft cast a spell on a half-circle of rapt boys with the tale of Achilles before the walls of Troy. Some of it Tetisheri recognized from Homer, the rest, especially the addition of Achilles' hand-to-hand battle with Ares over the favors of Aphrodite, was new to her and probably to everyone else on the street as well. An older woman with soulful dark eyes read fortunes in palms under the baleful surveillance of a Jewish priest with long earlocks.

There were cats wherever one looked, black, brown, white, striped tabbies and multicolored tortoiseshells. They begged the dairyman for milk and the fisherman for scraps. They twined around the ankles of the unwary, hissed at children who had the temerity to pull their tails, arched their backs and purred when their spines were scratched, pounced and played with a bit of string, and napped in the sun curled up on the wide ledge of a fountain or a half-wall of stone or a marble seat.

Roses bloomed everywhere, vying with bushes of rosemary and verbena and lavender to perfume the air. It was a city to delight every sense, and Tetisheri did not wonder at the dazed expressions of the visitors who wandered the streets.

Where a side street met the Soma a large wooden tray of artfully spilled unset gemstones perched on a sturdy metal tripod, towered over by two enormous guards armed with pilums, gladii, and long knives. Their job was to scowl menacingly in the background while the gem merchant, one Cordros, bargained deferentially with a young Alexandrian noble attired in silk tunic and kilt, who preened beneath a broad collar of gold and lapis beads and four broad beaten gold bracelets, one above and below each elbow. He was attended by ten or twelve of his closest friends, though none were as well dressed or as expensively adorned as he.

Tetisheri knew him and took care not to catch his eye. Cordros, a friend of Neb's, winked at her on the sly as she passed. "My lord, you wound me to the heart! My prices are the best you will find from here to Rome itself! Fifty denarii for such a stone would leave me no profit at all—"

"Nenwef still spending his wife's money as fast as her father hands it over to him, I see," Apollodorus said. "Our esteemed King Ptolemy did the girl no favors in arranging that marriage."

"Not so loud, you'll be heard."

"I don't care if I am."

A man, an upriver Egyptian by the look of his headscarf, was sent sprawling from the door of a taverna. Apollodorus stepped in between him and Tetisheri as the taverna keeper spat at their feet. "No Egyptians allowed! Keep out!"

Apollodorus helped the Egyptian to his feet. "All right there, sir?"

The Egyptian, dark face made darker by rage, wrenched out of Apollodorus' grip and shoved his way through the crowd. The Alexandrians and the tourists were largely indifferent, but across the street a group of Egyptians clustered and muttered together. Alexandria was a center of trade, scholarship, culture, and history, but beneath its glittering surface the city held its breath. For what? Until Caesar left? Until Ptolemy tried to kill Cleopatra and she killed him instead? Until the Egyptians rioted against their Greek lords? It had happened before, too many times to count.

Apollodorus watched the group of Egyptians until they noticed him looking and broke off to go their separate ways. "Who's the girl?" he said, continuing up the Way.

"What girl?"

"The young girl with the old eyes who answered the door."

"Oh. Keren."

"From Judea?"

"Yes."

"I thought so. All those dark curls. Another one of your runaways?"

"She wanted to be a doctor, not a wife. It wasn't an option her father was willing to entertain."

"How did she come your way?"

"Neb was homeward bound from Iskenderun almost two years ago. Someone told her to look for his sail and when he put into port at Jaffa to offload cargo, she stowed away on board. He didn't find her until he saw Pharos." She saw his smile from the corner of her eye and in spite of herself she smiled, too. "Well, all right. He didn't allow her to be found until then."

"What happened to the one before? The one from Persia who was fleeing a geriatric husband and his first three wives and their, what was it, twenty-four children?"

"Yasmin? Sosigenes took her on his staff."

Apollodorus' eyebrows went up. "On the staff of the queen's chief counselor? She did well for herself."

"She reads and writes Greek, Latin, and Persian, and he's teaching her cursive Demotic. He says she shows real aptitude. She took lodgings with Iphigenia to be nearer the Library."

"A scholar. I wonder how she managed that, given how cloistered the Persians keep their women."

"She says her father thought education was a way to keep the women quiet."

Apollodorus laughed out loud, a sound that had more than one woman look around and follow him with their eyes. "More fool he." He stepped out in front to lead the way through a knot of Roman tourists gathered around a display of allegedly antique pottery and statuary featuring the entire panoply of Egyptian gods and goddesses going all the way back, according to the lively, sharp-featured proprietor, to the First Dynasty. The Romans, displaying that touching reverence mixed with inferiority with which they approached all things pharaonic, looked only too willing to believe him.

"Poor bastards," Apollodorus said, still not bothering to lower his voice.

Tetisheri, knowing the proprietor, another and less savory friend of Uncle Neb's, agreed with him but she had other, more pressing things on her mind. "How is she?"

"Big as a hippo."

She quelled a giggle and tried to speak reprovingly. "This is not a respectful way of which to speak of our sovereign."

"She said it first." He glanced at her, a grin lurking at the corners of his mouth. The sun streaked his hair with gold. "Takes an extra large carpet to roll her up in these days."

She laughed outright at this and he paused in mid step, looking down at her. When Auletes had hired Apollodorus away from the Five Soldiers to be Auletes' daughter's personal bodyguard, Apollodorus had seemed so much older and more experienced. Now, he seemed oddly so much nearer in age and every bit as attractive as he had been when she was a moonstruck girl of twelve.

Her heart skipped a beat. "What?"

"Nothing," he said after a long moment in which she felt he spent an inordinate amount of time cataloguing features he already knew only too well. He moved on and she followed.

They passed still more docks facing the Great Harbor and still more shops and stalls and inns and tavernas that clustered opportunistically near the waterfront. They passed the obelisks, and the headquarters of the Queen's Guard, where the bellows of sergeants and the stamp of feet and clash of arms drowned out everything else. A smaller company of Egyptians, none of them over fourteen and indisputably new recruits, was being drilled with sword and shield. They were assisted in this effort by a voluntary critique from some off-duty Roman soldiers. If she read their insignia correctly, they were part of the Veteran Sixth Legion, the legion Caesar had brought with him which had suffered so many casualties in the late war.

"Put some shoulder into it, lad, it won't bite you," one of them said, and shook his head while the rest of his friends sighed and cast up their eyes when the recruit so advised hit himself in the head with the pommel of his own sword.

The sound of a sharp smack was followed by a yelp. The instructor drew his hand back for another blow, the round, slender stick in his hand whistling through the air to come down with another smack on the unlucky backside of the recruit nearest him. "Straighten up that line, you clumsy bastards! If your mothers could not teach you how to walk without tripping over your own feet, by Sobek's mighty balls the Royal Guard will!"

"I've never seen so many upriver folk under arms," Teti-sheri said.

"One of her new battalions," Apollodorus said. "She's been recruiting all the way up to Syrene and Philae."

"And they're actually coming?"

"They'll come for her."

"They wouldn't for Auletes."

He looked at her, brow raised. "No. But they will for her. She is their very own Isis made flesh, after all."

She knew what he meant. Four years before, they had both been present three hundred leagues up the river in Thebes when the queen had personally escorted the new Baucis bull to his home in the temple of Hermonthis (or Armant, as any Egyptian worshipper could and would tell you was its proper name). Every priest in Upper and Lower Egypt was present in full regalia and Cleopatra appeared larger than life beneath the Double Crown. All of them were attendant on the massive beast with the white body and the black face whose raiment nearly outshone the queen's. But only nearly.

Thousands of Egyptians had lined both shores of the Nile and crammed into boats large and small that so crowded the river you could have walked across it without getting your feet wet. They were there to cry out as one their adulation to the Lady of the Two Lands. Their collective religious fervor drove many to faint dead away into the arms of their companions, to be revived later by a feast at Cleopatra's expense which went on for days afterwards. It was a celebration to which the nomarchs in their annual reports to the crown attributed a dramatic uptick in births nine months later. All to the good, the queen would have said, as that meant more farmers, craftsmen and soldiers under arms nineteen years later.

Regardless, no one who was there ever forgot the sight— or neglected to say so over and over again—and no living Egyptian who had not attended more bitterly regretted any decision in their lives. Many of them were so struck by the queen's appearance at that event that they followed her downriver to Alexandria, where she welcomed them with a tithe of grain and a one-time relief from their annual tax to help them settle in.

In fact, Tetisheri thought, before Cleopatra took her place on the throne of the Ptolemies, Egyptians had formed less than a third of the population of Alexandria, a city dominated by the Macedonian Greek ruling class and supported by the Jewish population. Now they were moving in to the city themselves, settling down, selling their own goods directly instead of through Alexandrian middlemen, drinking in Alexandrian tavernas—or trying to—and training in Cleopatra's army.

Not everyone was comfortable with that change.

The extensive jumble of buildings that formed the Royal Palace gleamed richly in the noon sun, chiseled from limestone faced with marble and embellished with coral and lapis and turquoise and carnelian inlay. Elaborately carved columns supported bas-relief friezes depicting scenes from Atum creating Shu and Tefnut to Alexander scattering the grain that would become the de facto boundaries of the city, themselves painted every color of the rainbow. The mixture of dazzling white stone and garish rainbow paint was overwhelming, and when they entered through a small side door the relief was so abrupt Tetisheri closed her eyes for a moment to let them adjust. Apollodorus exchanged a nod with the guard, a grizzled Alexandrian Greek whose face she recognized but whose name she couldn't remember. She followed Apollodorus down a long hall with guards stationed an arm's length apart. They were, Tetisheri noted with interest, equally divided between Alexandrian Greeks and upriver Egyptians. To a man they looked narrow-eyed and suspicious, of Tetisheri and Apollodorus, and probably of each other as well.

Apollodorus went through another door and a series of connecting corridors less well attended, one of which went behind a false wall and another so dusty she was surprised at the absence of corpses, human and otherwise. Once she saw two slaves engaged in a furtive embrace in a dark corner, who broke apart and scurried off when they caught sight of Apollodorus and Tetisheri. Around another corner she saw a tall, thin man with dark hair cut in the Greek style in a nondescript tunic and sandals approaching from the direction they were going. She caught the impression of close-set eyes and a long, sharp nose before he vanished into a passage that might have led outside and just as easily might not have, she was so turned around. A self-important steward clutching a ring with many keys on it stood back deferentially when he saw Apollodorus, his head bent as they passed.

They emerged finally into a rectangular hall so large and bare of furnishings that their footsteps echoed off the walls. Apollodorus opened another door to reveal a short flight of stairs leading down. It was dark and airless and would have been intolerable if they had not emerged almost immediately onto another floor lit by torches. It must have been ventilated by hidden ducts because the flames flickered and the air was much fresher. Eventually they came to a door set deeply into the wall. Apollodorus knocked.

"Enter."

He opened the door and stepped back to let Tetisheri precede him.

In spite of being mostly underground the room had a quality of muted light, in part provided by long, narrow windows that lined the top of the exterior wall and admitted the salt tang of sea air and the sounds of waves lapping against rocks. Tetisheri thought the room must face the Royal Harbor and Pharos, and wondered if its light shone into this room at night.

It was a small, rectangular room. Shelves lined all four walls and were filled with a fascinating array of scrolls and wooden boxes and bowls of every size, shape and depth and large burlap sacks and tiny linen bags and a quantity of plain glass vials with cork stoppers, some of which were full of mysterious liquids and had been sealed with wax. Two long tables stood in the center of the room, their tops crowded with bowls and beakers and braziers. Everywhere there were strips of papyrus and scraps of vellum densely notated mostly—Tetisheri craned her neck—in Greek, but some in cursive Demotic as well.

A woman stood at the middle of one of the tables, tapping something from a square of papyrus into a bubbling pot set over a small brazier bearing a few glowing coals. "Thank you, Apollodorus," she said without looking up.

Tetisheri heard the door close behind her.

Cleopatra Philopater Thea Noetera, seventh of her name, seventeenth of her line (or possibly eighteenth, depending on whether or not you counted Ptolemy VII), the Lady of Two Lands, the incarnation on earth of the goddess Isis, and absolute ruler of Alexandria and Upper and Lower Egypt (unless you counted her brother and co-ruler, Ptolemy XIV, and no one did, unless you were Julius Caesar, in which case everyone else did, too), fed the now empty envelope to the hot coals and took up a small metal spoon on a long handle to stir the contents of the pot. Her shift was simple but woven of the finest linen. Her hair was dark except when the light caught a stray auburn gleam, and was held back from her face by a thin gold fillet in the Greek style.

"What are you working on?" Tetisheri said.

The queen watched the pot as it came back to a boil. "Dried powdered willow bark ground fine, pomegranate juice, and honey."

"What's it for?"

"A potion to ease menstrual cramps."

Tetisheri smiled. "Not something I would have thought you stood in need of at present."

"No," the queen said, chuckling as she ran a hand over her swollen belly. "Not just at present."

"You're big for five months."

"It's closer to six." Cleopatra sighed and rubbed her belly again. "But yes, very big. All the women in my family show early on, or so my aunt tells me."

The potion boiled high inside the pot and she stirred it down again. "I'm trying to come up with something that a woman can swallow without it making an immediate reappearance. The ancient texts agree that pomegranate reduces inflammations, and it certainly tastes better than any of the ingredients in the remedies Zotikos makes."

"They're that bad?"

The queen shuddered. "Which is what happens when you have a man brewing tinctures meant to be administered to women for women's problems."

Tetisheri grinned at the acid note in Cleopatra's voice. "And the honey? A binding agent?"

"So you weren't asleep during the entirety of Natan's classes after all. I often wondered. That, and the willow bark is so bitter and the pomegranate is so tart. I thought the honey might make it a little more palatable. Don't touch that."

Tetisheri's fingers had been hovering over a vial filled with some dark liquid. She snatched her hand back and looked up in inquiry.

"Enough and it heals," Cleopatra said. "Too much and it kills. Taken orally, almost instantly. Over time, used as a topical unguent, it can also prove fatal."

Tetisheri clasped her hands behind her back and maintained a respectful distance from everything in the room. "I knew you were skilled in potions and tinctures, Pati. I didn't know you'd branched out into poisons."

"I'm thinking of writing a pharmacopoeia. Merit-Ptah could do with some updating." The queen covered the coals in the brazier and looked up. Her wide-spaced eyes were large and dark and thickly lashed, her nose long, her mouth wide and full-lipped, her chin strong. She wasn't pretty, exactly, but there was an animated quality about every breath she took that drew attention and kept it. When Cleopatra Philopator caught your eye, you didn't look away. "It's been a long time, Sheri."

"Well, you've been busy, Pati."

"That I have. And you?"

"The business flourishes. Uncle Neb is just back from

upriver. I left him gloating over his newest boatload of treasures."

Cleopatra raised an eyebrow. "Did he bring back any books?"

Tetisheri laughed. "It would be as much as my life was worth if I told you that he had."

With mock severity the queen said, "Are you implying I'm in the habit of commandeering trade goods legally acquired by my citizens?"

"I'm implying nothing, I'm stating a fact." Tetisheri let their mutual laughter warm her for a moment. But only for a moment. "Not that I'm not happy to see you, Pati, but why am I here?"

Cleopatra stretched, rubbing her knuckles into the base of her spine, before opening the drawer of a small chest sitting on one of the shelves. She removed a small round, flat object and tossed it to Tetisheri.

Tetisheri had to fall back a step but she caught it neatly in her right hand. "Wouldn't we have looked the idiots if I'd missed," she said with some asperity, "crawling around on the floor looking for it."

"Queens don't crawl around on the floor," Cleopatra said with her nose in the air. "We have minions who crawl for us." She nodded. "Take a look."

It was a coin, a brand new bronze coin, images clear, edges unworn, very shiny. On one side was a strongly drawn image of Isis suckling Horus. "Horus," said Tetisheri. "You're very sure. Because Caesar must have a son?"

The queen winced and rubbed her belly again. "No, because this one is trying out for the Olympics before he's even out of the womb."

On the other side of the coin was a monogram shaped like a tree, with Cleopatra's name and title spelled out around the rim. "Cyprus?"

The queen nodded. "We strike all our new coins there."

"A new drachma?"

The queen nodded.

"That's the second in two years."

"I have to do something, Sheri. There hasn't been an adequate supply of coins in circulation since Ptolemy X. If there is no coin to spend no one can buy, and that is not a recipe for a stable economy in the largest port on the Middle Sea."

"Most of the coin we see is silver."

Cleopatra nodded. "And Roman. You don't have to say it, Sheri, I know."

"So." Tetisheri tossed the coin back and Cleopatra caught it every bit as neatly as Tetisheri had. "A new issue. A nice likeness, too, Oh Great Isis. I don't know whether to bow or just abase myself before your image and be done with it."

Cleopatra's smile was only perfunctory. Tetisheri cocked her head. "What's wrong, Pati?"

"Walk with me," the queen said, and Tetisheri followed her out the door, Apollodorus falling in behind them. They went down the corridor, up some stairs, down another corridor, and up some more stairs to emerge onto a small balcony that overlooked the Royal Harbor. Pharos stood tall and proud across the mouth of the harbor, ready to light the way home when night fell. For now the cataract of sunlight flooded the shadows so that the warren of buildings that made up the palace seemed flattened, as if they were a two-dimensional map of themselves.

A striped awning had been unrolled to shade the balcony. There was a small table bearing a pitcher and glasses and a tray of bread and fruit and cheese. "Sit," the queen said. Tetisheri and Apollodorus sat while the queen poured.

Tetisheri accepted a glass and a bit of cheese and sat. The juice was cold and of some pleasing mixture of citrus sweetened with honey. The cheese was velvety smooth and slightly tart. The rounds of bread were still warm from the oven. For a moment the three of them ate and drank and admired the view. It was an oddly peaceful one, as land and seascape both were relatively deserted as Alexandrians broke their fast under shelter from the heat of midday. Even the gulls were silent.

The queen licked her fingers clean and drained her glass and set it down. "The first shipment of the new coinage went missing five days ago."

Tetisheri, who had been on the alert since the queen had served them with her own hands, said, "How unfortunate." She was unable to keep her tone wholly free of suspicion.

Cleopatra's smile was wide and knowing and utterly charming. "How carefully disinterested you sound, my dear Sheri."

"And how well you wear that cobra on your forehead,

Pati," Tetisheri said, and then cast an involuntary look over her shoulder. It was one thing to revert to childhood nicknames behind closed doors, and another entirely to use them where anyone might hear.

"Don't worry, Iras and Charmion have instructions to ensure our privacy." Cleopatra's smile faded. "I tasked my Eye with finding the lost shipment."

Tetisheri felt a sense of growing dread. "Not Aristander?"

"He knows, but in his office he is constrained to answer also to my brother." The words "at present" were unsaid but felt by all three of them.

"And?" Tetisheri said.

Cleopatra looked at Apollodorus. "And the Eye was murdered very early this morning," he said. "Near the Eunostos docks. Not too far from Neb's warehouse, as it happens."

Tetisheri did not make the mistake of imagining for one moment the queen had called her into her presence to accuse her of the crime. They had known each other far too long and too well. No, the queen had something else in mind and unfortunately, Tetisheri was horribly afraid she knew what it was. "Pati—"

The queen's expression was inexorable. "We have to find that shipment, Sheri, and we have to find it immediately. I've already commissioned another issue but the people who stole the first can hide it away and start spending it when the second issue is in circulation, which will only lower the face value of both and upset Alexandria's trade further. The plan was to exchange the old coin for the new, slowly, carefully, so there was no panic, so that the new currency has time to build in value and the old doesn't lose its value too quickly. Remember what Sosigenes taught us when we were studying the ancient Greeks? Too much new currency dumped all at once into the marketplace is as destabilizing to an economy as too little."

Her eyes narrowed and her voice deepened. "And even if I had the new coins with me in the Royal Palace right now, every last one of them under lock and key, murder has been done. Murder, here in Alexandria, bloody murder of an Alexandrian citizen, and further, of one of my closest and most valuable servants. This cannot, this may not, go undiscovered, or unpunished."

"I agree, of course I do. But I'm not—"

"Apollodorus will aid you in your investigation. The body is with the Shurta, and Aristander has promised me personally that unless he is asked, he will volunteer no information about the murder or the investigation. To anyone. Other than yourselves."

Tetisheri closed her eyes. "Please don't ask this of me."

Cleopatra leaned forward and slipped her hand into Tetisheri's. It felt smooth and strong and warm. So did the drachma she pressed into Tetisheri's palm. The Eye she handed her openly. It did not feel nearly so warm to the touch. "There is no one but you I can ask this of, Tetisheri. I am surrounded by spies set in place by the Romans, by the nobles, by my brother, all of whom are watching and waiting for me to make that one slip so they can push me the rest of the way over the edge and applaud as I fall. If those coins are not found, this could be that slip."

She would have said more when Charmion slipped out onto the balcony, gave Tetisheri a quick nod, and whispered something into the queen's ear. The queen was instantly on her feet and in motion, prodigiously pregnant or not. "Tell her, Apollodorus. Tell her everything. She is to have immediate and unquestioned access to whatever she needs. Find the coin, find the thieves, and find the killer and bring all to me."

"On the floor," Charmion hissed. There was the sound of feet that sounded very much like soldiers marching. Tetisheri and Apollodorus both went from chair to knees in one motion, their foreheads pressed to the cool marble. Tetisheri slipped the drachma into the purse at her waist just in time.

"Ah, lovey, I was just in search of you." The male voice was hoarse and a trifle high. Tetisheri, peeking over her arm, saw a tall man, a little thick with age around the middle, dressed in a white tunic with a purple hem. He had a beaky nose and his hair was combed forward to cover his bald spot. His scalp shone pinkly through the scant iron gray strands nonetheless.

Cleopatra's voice was indulgent and more than a little suggestive. "And how may I serve the mighty Caesar?"

There was a loud smack, and after a stupefied moment Tetisheri realized that Julius Caesar had just slapped Cleopatra Philopator, the Lady of the Two Lands, seventh of her name, seventeenth in her line and the incarnation of Isis on the earth, on her behind. "You may get yourself to your bed, lady, and myself after you. We don't have much time left to play, you and I."

"Your son may take exception to that, my Caesar."

A loud, neighing laugh. "My son will one day be a man and understand, my queen."

This was more than Tetisheri ever wanted to know about her queen's private life, and at the same time she had to stifle a highly inappropriate giggle. She sneaked a look to her side. Apollodorus had his forehead on his hands and his behind in the air, which prompted another stifled giggle.

"Who have we here?" Sandal-clad feet stopped in front of Tetisheri, and a dry hand reached beneath her chin and raised her inexorably to her feet. Dark, piercing eyes gave her a thorough and comprehensive look and warmed to what they saw. "Jupiter, look at those eyes. As blue as the sky at morning. And who might you be?"

"The one tasked with cooking your supper this evening, mighty Caesar, so if you don't want her to poison the soup I suggest you let her be about her business." Cleopatra nodded at Tetisheri, who abased herself before her queen once more before getting to her feet. She tried not to hurry herself out of their presence, not entirely successfully. "Apollodorus, to your station."

"My queen."

In the doorway Tetisheri nearly bumped into a second Roman, near to Caesar in age, his tunic white but without the purple trim, tall and with no spare ounce of flesh about his person. A long face descended from a high forehead that went all the way back to the nape of his neck. The hollows in his cheeks were cavernous, his lips a thin, clamped line. His deep-set eyes were dark, and his burning gaze was fixed on the queen. In the brief glimpse she had of him Tetisheri could not tell if that gaze said more of disapproval or desire.

She slipped past him, only to trip over a third Roman in the hallway. This one was of an age with the first two but a little shorter and with more hair. He was dressed in a simple tunic belted at the waist, but the confident set of his shoulders and the proud carriage of his head said soldier.

Impersonal hands caught her by the shoulders before she fell and released her the moment she regained her balance. Their eyes met and held for a brief moment, hers startled, his at first indifferent and then intent. She looked away and continued down the hall.

The great scar that notched the left side of his forehead betrayed his identity. Cotta, that would be, Caesar's cousin who had been with him since Gaul. It was in Gaul, it was said, that Cotta had deliberately caught the killing blow by an Arveni chieftain meant for Caesar.

There was no more trusted member of Caesar's retinue. Rumor had it he would be left behind when Caesar departed, stationed in Alexandria, ostensibly as Roman legate to the Alexandrian crown but really to safeguard Caesar's interests in the Nile's annual grain crops.

Anyone who wanted a Roman triumph needed first of all bread made from Egyptian grain to feed the Roman rabble, and second, Egyptian gold to sweeten the Roman Senate.

3

on the afternoon of the Tenth Day of the Second Week
at the Eighth Hour...

The Shurta, Alexandria's local police force, was housed
in a large rectangular building set back from the
Canopic Way. Its frontage had no paint of any color
whatsoever to mar the single dignified row of columns below
or highlight the absence of a frieze above. This severe lack of
ostentation was in stark contrast to the gloriously detailed
peacocks of the main building of the Great Library and the
Soma to either side and to the Dicasterium across the Way.
Its very reticence rather drew the eye than elided it. At any
rate, no citizen of Alexandria or visitor thereof was in doubt
as to the service the building housed, and care was taken
by everyone of any station or origin not to catch the eye of
the guards posted in front. Even the long-legged ibises that
stalked the cross streets begging for crumbs seemed to avoid

that section of the Way. The Shurta's reputation for probity and efficiency stood out in a nation whose bureaucracy was otherwise infamous for graft and bribery.

A young officer, correct in uniform and discreet in demeanor, murmured, "This way, please," when Apollodorus gave his name and said Aristander was expecting them. He brought them to a long, narrow room containing a long wooden table. Beneath it a deep, central gutter ran from west wall to east. A slave in a shenti and nothing else washed blood and small, unidentifiable bits and pieces down the gutter with a broom and buckets of water. The gutter emptied through the hole in the eastern wall, where its contents could be heard rushing down a pipe to somewhere else—one hoped the central sewer which emptied into the sea and not Lake Mareotis, which was where the city's drinking water came from.

The room was cool and dim and a large cone of incense burned in every corner, the smoke drifting upwards to vent through holes in the three exterior walls just beneath the ceiling. It took most of the noxious smells with it and a good thing, too, since other tables were occupied by bodies sewn into shrouds prior to being transferred to the embalmers and the priests for the tomb or the pot.

"Tetisheri!" A slim man with bright brown eyes hurried forward with his hands outstretched. "It has been too long since we have met."

She accepted his hands in her own and regarded him with affection. "It has at that, Aristander. You are well? Merti? The children?"

He beamed. "They are all well, and would love to see you." He dropped her hands and his face sobered. "I'm happy to see you, but I am sorry for the circumstances that brought us together today. A less auspicious occasion could hardly be imagined."

She remembered then that Aristander was a religious man. The figure of Maat on his pectoral was not only the badge of his office as the head of the Shurta but the image of the goddess of truth, justice, and morality he worshipped daily and sacrificed to every feast day. "You know why I'm here," she said.

"Yes, this way." He led them to a table in the back, the figure of a woman discernible beneath a length of linen. "Idut, if you please."

The morgue attendant stepped to the head of the table and drew back the cloth.

"Khemit?" Tetisheri said.

Apollodorus was surprised. "You didn't know?"

She cast a warning glance at Idut, and Aristander motioned the man out of earshot. "I think that's the point of the position," she said in a low voice. "Only the queen knows the identity of the Eye." She looked back at the body.

Khemit had been in her late fifties, thin to the point of gauntness, and gifted by the gods with a ceaseless energy that Tetisheri and the rest of Alexandria—save two: the queen and Khemit's murderer—thought had been expended in overseeing the successful weaving business she owned near the Western Gate, the area where most of Alexandria's weavers clustered together. Tetisheri had bought all her household linens there, and knew Khemit as a woman never too busy to greet a customer by name and not too proud to untangle a novice weaver's reversal of warp and weft. They had known each other as seller and buyer but they had never socialized. Khemit lived in Rhakotis and Tetisheri on the waterfront, Khemit was all Greek and Tetisheri only half, there were at least thirty years between them, and their paths had crossed only on business. Tetisheri had known Cleopatra all of her life and had never once seen the queen and Khemit together. That in all that time she had heard no whisper of Khemit's other line of work only added to the mystique of the Queen's Eye.

Khemit frowned in death, eyebrows drawn together, mouth pulled into a scowl. "She looks angry."

Aristander looked at the dead woman's face. "Why, so she does. I hadn't noticed."

"And... dark?" Khemit's face was several shades darker than when Tetisheri had last seen her alive.

"Yes, she fell face down. The blood pools in the lowest parts of the body after death. She wasn't discovered until sunrise and she was cool by then, but her body had not yet stiffened so I would estimate she had been dead for less than twelve hours. She began to stiffen after she was brought here—I had Idut check every half hour. My best guess is she was killed near the Twentieth Hour, but it is just that, only a guess."

"Who found her?"

"A street sweeper. He came to us at once. I am confident he knows nothing of the circumstances around her death."

"How was she killed?"

"A blow to the head." Aristander slid his hands beneath Khemit's head and raised it to show them. All of Khemit's body came up with her, her form rigid from head to toe. He turned the body on its side, facing him, and pointed. "You see the depression in the skull there?"

They could hardly miss it. The blow had struck hard enough to leave the skull misshapen. Khemit's hair was matted with dried blood and gray matter.

"Right side," Apollodorus said. "The killer was right-handed?"

"Perhaps just an expert who knew where he had to strike, and how hard," Aristander said. "It would depend on which side the killer attacked from."

Tetisheri swallowed hard. "Was she harmed in any other way?"

Aristander shook his head. "The blow to the head only."

"And the weapon?"

"A club or a stick of some kind," Aristander said. "A sword or an axe would have cleaved the skull, not broken it."

"Did you find anything unusual upon her person? Something she might not ordinarily be carrying?"

Aristander glanced at Idut and lowered his voice. "Only the Eye."

"Who else saw it?"

He laid the body back down with gentle hands. "Idut

here was alone on duty when the street sweeper arrived. He described the Eye, hanging from her neck by a chain. Idut knew immediately what it was. He went from here to my home and from there we went directly to where her body lay. No other than Idut and myself have touched her. Other than myself, only the streetsweeper and Idut have seen the body. Only Idut saw the Eye. I have sworn both to secrecy."

Tetisheri picked up the piece of linen and smoothed it back over Khemit's body. "Is this wound similar to others you have seen, Aristander?"

"It is," he said, "and it isn't. For one thing, I can't say for sure that whoever struck the blow meant to kill."

"But—"

"Someone meant to hit her, Sheri," Apollodorus said. "But that someone may not have meant to kill her."

"If they hadn't meant to kill her, why strike her down?"

"It was a blow of great force, agreed."

"It certainly looks like deliberate murder," Aristander said, nodding. "But it is entirely too soon to be making assumptions. As yet, the only evidence we have is the body." He paused. "We can rule out theft, certainly. The only thing of value on her body was the Eye, and no self-respecting thief would have left that behind."

It was even possible, Tetisheri thought, that the Eye had been left behind deliberately as a message to Khemit's mistress as a warning against further investigation. *See what happens when you send your servant to inquire too closely into my business?* If that were the case, the killer didn't know Cleopatra very well, which could be a clue to his identity all on its own. "What was she doing out on the streets of the city at the Twentieth Hour?"

"I would guess she was about her mistress' business," Aristander said.

"And that business got her killed," Apollodorus said.

Aristander raised a hand. "Perhaps."

Apollodorus smiled. "Ever cautious, Aristander. Very well. Perhaps."

Aristander escorted them to the main door and took a fond leave of Tetisheri and a respectful one of Apollodorus. They emerged into the sunlight and Tetisheri took a deep breath of air that smelled only of salt water and the wood fire from the cart nearest the corner, where someone was roasting kebabs of goat meat interspersed with onion and peppers. A wave of nausea and dizziness came over her and she swayed on her feet.

"Oh no you don't." Apollodorus slid his arm around her waist and half walked, half carried her across the street to where someone else was squeezing juice from pomegranates cooled by a block of ice brought down the river from the mountains far to the south. He purchased cups for both of them and then moved her to the edge of one of the many fountains and pools that lined the center of the Way.

The cool spray of the fountain was refreshing and the juice was tart and cool. Slowly, Tetisheri recovered her composure. "Thank you. I don't know what came over me."

"I'd wager that was the first time you saw a body done to death by violence," Apollodorus said. "That would do for anyone, I would think." He paused. "You did well."

"I almost fainted in there," she said with asperity.

"No, you almost fainted out here. There's a difference."

"If you say so."

"Keeping control in the moment and letting down your guard after the fact are two different things. The former is essential. The latter is understandable and possibly even necessary. You held it together when it mattered. I'm impressed."

"Well. If you're impressed."

She could hear the smile in his voice. "Finish your juice and we'll go talk to the captain of the ship the coin came in on."

Surprised, she said, "Aristander doesn't have him in custody?"

He looked at her.

Oh. Of course. If Aristander had the captain in custody he would perforce have to allow access to him by both co-regnants. "Ah," she said. "Shall we?"

"You're joking," she said.

They were standing on a long wharf near the Heptastadion. A dozen ships of various sizes and conditions were moored to both sides. The ship before them was a deep-hulled merchant galley. The top half of an improbably buxom woman carved from wood was fixed to the prow and the weight of gold leaf applied to her skin probably lowered the front half of the ship by at least two fingers. There was a large piece of anonymous equipment amidships with a tarp lashed over it. A winch, perhaps, or some other device designed to aid in the swift loading and unloading of cargo.

The galley bore a single, three-cornered sail now furled to a crosspiece fixed to the mast. Tetisheri had seen many ships rigged like this one on a journey to Punt with Uncle Neb, but this was the first time she'd seen one in the Middle Sea. "This is the ship?"

Apollodorus nodded.

"Where are the ports for the sweeps?"

"She isn't oared."

She turned to stare at him. "No rowers?"

He shook his head.

"But—but that's insane, Apollodorus. What about pirates?"

"She outruns them."

"And that's fine if there is a fair wind," Tetisheri said with awful sarcasm, "but if she is becalmed?"

"Her captain takes care that she is not," Apollodorus said, and he kept a straight face while he said it.

Tetisheri closed her eyes and shook her head. "The man is mad. And the queen is mad for trusting him on such a mission."

He didn't answer her, but there was just the hint of a smile at the corners of his mouth. She could see nothing about this situation that anyone would find amusing but it was apparent he wasn't going to enlighten her. "Well." Tetisheri blew out a breath. "She looks seaworthy, at any rate. Two hundred fifty tons?"

Apollodorus nodded.

Tetisheri eyed the trim lines of the sleek little vessel. "She does have the appearance of a ship that eats the leagues port to port," she said grudgingly.

"Her missions are never ones for dawdling."

Tetisheri gave him a suspicious look, but Apollodorus presented a blank countenance which refused to give anything away.

There were two men on the deck in civilian clothes that nevertheless screamed "guard" in the sharp eyes that missed nothing and the well-cared-for weapons at their sides. They were longtime members of the queen's personal guard and Tetisheri knew both of them by sight. "You have him locked up on his own ship?"

"It's the last place anyone would think to look, isn't it?" He saw her skepticism. "Besides, it's not like you can hide anyone or anything away for long in this town. This was the best I could do."

"Does Aristander know?"

"Only the queen. Aristander knows nothing about the theft of the currency. Only the queen and Sosigenes. And now us."

"And the crew of this ship?"

"Obviously, they would have loaded the chests, and would probably have suspected from the weight that what was inside must be valuable. But no one told them, unless the captain knew, and did."

She contemplated Apollodorus, the two guards and the ship, and sighed. "Let's go ask him."

He offered his hand. She ignored it, stepping nimbly from wharf to railing and down onto the ship's deck, no assistance required, thank you. He might have been grinning as he followed her.

The niece and partner of a merchant trader, most of whose goods were carried in the holds of ships they owned, Tetisheri knew a well-maintained vessel when she saw one and she was looking at one now. The deck was scrubbed clean, the sail was neatly folded and bound, the lines were coiled. Rudjek and Pentu, the guards, nodded at both of them without speaking. The runners on the hatch that led below-decks were well waxed so that the hatch slid open without hesitation.

The captain, too, was unexpected. He sat splicing an eye into the end of a mooring line. He looked up as they descended the short ladder into the galley.

"Ah, Apollodorus, back again," he said, without any trace of alarm, or of guilt that Tetisheri could detect. "And you brought a friend with you this time, I see. How nice." He gave Tetisheri an appreciative look and a smile that was friendly without being in any way ingratiating. He was the least alarmed person suspected of a crime punishable by death that Tetisheri could imagine. "Introduce us, why don't you?"

"She is an agent of the queen. That is all you need to know."

"Pity." The captain executed a half bow from his seated position. "Laogonus, owner and captain of the good ship *Thalassa*, at your service. Please." He waved a hand. "Have a seat. May I offer you some tea?"

"Thank you, no." Tetisheri was determined to match the good captain in insouciance in this, her very first interrogation. "Captain Laogonus, will you please repeat the events that led up to the, ah, disappearance of your cargo? All of them."

"From the time we left Alexandria?" He glanced at Apollodorus.

"From the time you loaded your cargo on Lemesos," Apollodorus said.

"No," Tetisheri said firmly. "Begin with when you were first assigned to carry the cargo from Lemesos to Alexandria."

At minimum she was pleased to see that she had startled the captain out of his unshakeable calm. "What?"

"You heard her," Apollodorus said.

Laogonus hesitated, looking from one to the other, and set the rope and spike to one side. "Very well." He spoke without hesitation but neither did Tetisheri get the feeling he had rehearsed what he had to say. He told his story chronologically and with at least no outward sign of internal editing.

He'd had his orders, he said, from Sosigenes. He had met him here, on board *Thalassa*, and given him his instructions and the name of the agent he was to contact in Lemesos, one Paulinos Longinus.

"When was this?"

"The Ninth Day of the First Week."

"And you were to depart Alexandria when?"

"The next day at first light."

Eleven days ago. "Was anyone else present when Sosigenes gave you your orders?"

Laogonus shook his head. "Sosigenes came here alone and asked me to order the crew ashore." He shrugged. "There was only Old Pert, who was happy enough to adjourn to his daughter's taverna for an hour or two."

"Where was the rest of your crew?"

"We had just returned from Ephesus and I'd given them leave. Old Pert is a widower and his children grown so he makes his home here on *Thalassa*."

"So the vessel is never left unmanned."

"No." Laogonus spoke with emphasis. "Not here in Alexandria and never in a foreign port. That's just begging for trouble."

It was Uncle Neb's standard practice as well. "So you left Alexandria the Tenth Day of First Week at dawn."

He nodded. "I had the city launch tow us from the harbor and we were lucky enough to pick up the first of the offshore winds. We cranked on sail and were in Lemesos by noon of Second Day of Second Week."

Eight days ago. Even with a fair wind, with a single sail and no oarsmen, that was good time. "How long were you in port before you made contact with the agent?"

"He was waiting for us at the docks."

"Was he? With your cargo?"

"Yes. We loaded it immediately and left as soon as we had it secured in the hold."

"You didn't stop to take on supplies? Have a drink? Visit your girlfriend?"

He chuckled. "I see you are wise to the ways of sailors, ma'am."

"You see correctly. And so?"

He shook his head. "We met Paulinos, took on the cargo, and set sail for Alexandria immediately. I would say within the hour but it was even sooner than that."

"What was the cargo?"

"Twenty small wooden chests, locked and lashed."

"How had Longinus brought them to the wharf in Lemesos?"

"By donkey train."

"Did you know what was inside the chests?"

"No."

"Did you ask?"

"No. I never ask on this kind of shipment."

"'This kind of shipment'?"

He smiled. "Any cargo contracted by the crown."

"You've carried such shipments before?"

He shrugged.

Tetisheri looked at Apollodorus, her eyes narrowed. "That doesn't answer my question, Captain."

His eyes twinkled. He did everything but grin at her. "The chests were very heavy for something so small."

She waited. So did he. She sighed. "What next?"

"The winds were with us, even more so than when we were northward bound, and we sighted Pharos after dark on the Fourth Day. We followed it in and docked at the Twenty-first Hour. I kept the crew on board until the following morning while I went to tell Sosigenes his cargo was in."

"What happened?"

He sighed, and looked at Apollodorus. "Everything?"

"Everything."

"Very well." Laogonus met Tetisheri's eyes with a steady gaze from which all trace of former amusement had been banished. "We were not the only ship to dock late that night. A second followed us in. The wharf was crowded and the port master rafted them next to us until the next day when, he said, he could sort us out by daylight. I didn't like it, but it happens, and if I'd made a fuss it would have drawn attention, and the whole point of our existence is to not draw attention." He shook his head. "At first light I was on my way to let Sosigenes know we had made port and to send for the cargo." His lips tightened. "The moment I was out of sight, an extremely fortuitous fire began in the ship that docked after us. Standard practice in Alexandria port—in any well-run port, for that matter—is for the burning vessel to be cut loose before the fire jumps ships."

Or to shore, Tetisheri thought. Alexandrians shared a vivid memory of the year before when Caesar had set fire to his ships and that fire had leapt ashore, nearly wiping out the buildings of the Royal Palace and the Great Library.

"Instead," Laogonus said, "someone cut our lines. By the time my crew realized it both ships, still lashed together, had drifted into the middle of the harbor, and the firefighters on the pilot boat had to fight early morning traffic to get to us."

"And then?"

He snorted. "And then my crew was attacked by the crew of the burning ship. They were all of them injured, none seriously, thank the gods."

"What happened next?"

The captain's smile was mirthless. "By what the port master has managed to piece together from various people watching from the shore, the *Thalassa* was swarmed by a series of rowboats, one after the other. From land, it looked as if they were offering help, debarking the crews, when in reality they were offloading the cargo. After which they all rowed off in different directions." His voice rose, betraying his first sign of anger. "They didn't even bother to sever the lines between *Thalassa* and the burning ship, they left them both to sink and burn." His big scarred hands clenched together on the galley table. In a calmer voice he said, "If Old Pert didn't have the hardest head this side of the Middle Sea she would have sunk with the other one. But he regained consciousness in time to break out the axe and cut the lines, and the pilot boat towed us back to the wharf. Which was when I arrived back on the scene."

"It happened very fast," Tetisheri said. "It doesn't take that long to walk to the palace and back again."

He did not bridle at the implication. "The theft was well planned and extremely well executed."

"Has anything like this happened before?"

"Never." There was no room for equivocation in the flat statement.

"What happened to the burned ship?"

"At the bottom of the harbor. The port master is worried that it will be a hazard to navigation, so he's sending divers down to clear the wreckage when he can find a moment that won't disrupt traffic, whenever that may be. We may learn something from that, but I wouldn't bet on it. These people seem to have covered their tracks very tidily." That last statement was entirely lacking in admiration.

They sat in silence for a few moments. "Is there anything else you can tell us, Captain Laogonus?" Tetisheri said finally. "Any detail, no matter how trivial, might be of use."

He frowned down at his still clenched fists. "I've been trying to remember anything I can about the ship that burned. We were all tired and, as I said, it is part of our mandate that we are to draw no attention to ourselves. I exchanged greetings with someone who said he was the captain but he didn't give his name—neither did I—and the moon had already set so it was pitch dark. I didn't get a good look at him or his crew or his ship. They were smaller than we were, I think." He shook his head. "Difficult to be sure."

"Who took first watch?"

"I did." A glint of returning amusement showed in his eyes. "Quick passages are always strenuous and I told the crew to rack out."

"Second watch?"

"None. I kept watch for the rest of the night. It was only a few hours and I planned to sleep long and well once we unloaded the cargo."

"Who did you wake before you left the ship?"

"Dedu, my first mate."

"How many in your crew?"

"Five, and before you ask, they have all been with me since I bought the *Thalassa*."

"When was that?"

"Twelve years ago this coming Hathyr."

"Prior to this one, how many of these, ah, missions have you completed?"

Laogonus looked at Apollodorus, who raised an eyebrow. The captain shrugged. "They are the only missions I do, mistress. The queen loaned me the money to buy the *Thalassa*, and in return I work only for her."

That didn't answer her question, exactly, but it was enough. Tetisheri rose to her feet. "Thank you, Captain, I think that's all for now. I may have more questions for you later."

He followed them up on deck. "I'm not going anywhere.

We've only just completed our repairs, and I have a diver scheduled to sound *Thalassa*'s hull this afternoon. Just as a precaution." He looked over the harbor side of the ship and they came up beside him. Two of the cedar planks looked brand new and others bore faint burn marks, planed away for the most part and gleaming with newly applied varnish. Tetisheri ran her fingers over a fresh, deep cut on the railing and the captain said, "I understand his enthusiasm at the time but I could wish Old Pert swung a less zealous axe. We'll have to replace the railing at some point." He contemplated the scar for a moment. "Although I don't know. Perhaps we should leave it as a warning not to let unknown ships tie up next to us in future. No matter what the port master says."

Once they were walking back up the wharf Tetisheri said, "Those guards are not there to keep Laogonus from escaping. They are there to guard his life."

"Yes."

"You might have mentioned how high he stands in the queen's trust."

Apollodorus seemed to choose his words carefully. "She would prefer that I did not." And then he changed the subject. "Where to next?"

"Do you know where Khemit lived?"

"Over the shop."

"Then we go there."

4

on the evening of the Tenth Day
of the Second Week at the
Tenth Hour...

The loft above Khemit's workshop was light and airy and almost spartan in its lack of furnishings. There was a couch, a bed, a cupboard with one shelf for sheets and towels and another for a small collection of garments. Two pairs of sandals, plain but of good manufacture, were lined up to one side of the cupboard. A long, high table pushed against one wall held a pitcher and a basin made of glazed clay, and one cup and one bowl made of red clay. It appeared that Khemit hadn't entertained much.

There were two other items only in the room. One was a small loom, the top pegged to the wall, the rods and shuttles placed as if Khemit had only just set them down. The weaving she had been working on was barely begun, the threads dyed in rich colors, one gold. The weaving showed two feet clad in jeweled sandals and above them what was logically the hem of a kilt or a tunic. "Did she always work from the bottom up?"

"Not always, but often enough not to occasion comment. She told me once that it was like solving a mystery, working upwards to discover the faces."

Tetisheri wondered if weaving from the bottom up worked as a metaphor for the work Khemit undertook for the queen. It wasn't a bad one.

Near the door was an ebony altar, small but beautifully carved and gleaming with polish. The stub of a candle sat in front. Arranged in a semicircle around it were the miniature figures of Maat, Bast, and a third god Tetisheri did not recognize. She pointed. "Who is this?"

Tarset, Khemit's chief assistant, was a woman in her forties who held herself erect, hands clasped tightly in front of her. "That is Nit. The goddess of weaving. See the shuttle in her hands?"

Looking more closely at the little figure, the lines of the shuttle became clearer. "I've never heard of her."

Tarset's face relaxed for a moment. "Not so surprising given that we Egyptians have been inventing new gods for four thousand years."

Tetisheri smiled. "True enough. Was Khemit so devout, then?"

"Well." Tarset frowned, considering. "She was a very private person, and one did not see much of her outside the shop. But, yes, she attended the public functions at the temple of Isis on Pharos. The entire staff did, and then would return here for wine and cakes. All at her expense, I might add."

"She was a good mistress then."

"Very."

"She had no family?"

"She never spoke of any, and none came to visit in the fifteen years that I've been here."

"Who inherits the shop?"

"She left it to me and to the other workers." The older woman's eyes filled with tears and she looked away, taking deep, measured breaths. "We've all been with her for years, and her scribe came today to tell us the news."

"How did the scribe learn of her death?"

"I stopped at his office on my way to you," Apollodorus said. "At the queen's command."

A tear rolled down Tarset's cheek. She wiped it away with a corner of her robe. "He said she wanted to provide for us, for our continued support."

"I'm glad for you, Tarset, and for all the women here."

"If there is an afterlife and Nit does truly exist there, Khemit will sit at her right hand for all eternity." The other woman's expression seemed to say that the goddess would do well to heed Tarset's wishes.

"No doubt." Tetisheri paused. "Did Khemit have any unusual visitors over, say, the past week?"

"Unusual?" Tarset looked taken aback. "Do you mean other than people coming to buy? No."

"Did she have any enemies that you know of? Anyone who took her in dislike? An unhappy customer, perhaps?"

Tarset drew herself up to her full height and did her best to look down her nose at Tetisheri, who stood a full hand taller. "Certainly not. Khemit's Fine Linens always provides perfect satisfaction."

"Of course," Tetisheri murmured. She saw a shift in Tarset's expression. "Yes?"

"Well." Tarset hesitated. "There was the one gentleman who came in on, oh, Seventh Day of last week? I didn't catch his name but he was a Greek."

"Did you recognize him? Was he a regular customer?"

Tarset made a face. "It is sometimes difficult to tell one Alexandrian noble from another. From the moment of their births everything has been given to them, and they have no reason to expect everything will not continue to be given." Her lips tightened. "This one was much the same. He marched into the shop as if he owned it and demanded to speak with Khemit in private that very moment. She wanted no fuss made in front of the other customers—there was a rich Roman who was placing a large order of fine linens to be shipped to Rome—so she took him into the back room."

"What was his complaint?"

Tarset made a dismissive gesture. "We could hear their voices from the shop but not the words."

"Do you remember what he looked like? Can you give us a description?"

"Young, slim, arrogant." Tarset dismissed him with a shrug.

"Nothing else?"

"I can certainly describe his attire." Tarset made a face. "Gaudy. No style or taste. Fah."

"How so?"

"He wore bracelets from wrist to elbow on both arms, a gold inlay collar that reached to his breastbone, and earrings that will stretch his earlobes to his shoulders before he is thirty if he's not careful. His tunic was heavily embroidered in gold and silver thread and I don't know how he managed to walk in sandals so encrusted with gemstones."

"Would you recognize him again?"

"I would certainly recognize those sandals," Tarset said, rolling her eyes. "We all would. But Atet might remember his face. She admitted him."

"Atet?" Tetisheri said, surprised and pleased. "Atet is still with you?"

"No." Tarset smiled. "She has now married and moved out of the city."

"Did she! I wish I had known, I would have sent a gift."

"It was very sudden."

"Sudden?"

"She left us only two days ago." Tarset smiled, only to have it fade. "It was good that she was gone before the news came of Khemit. They were very fond of each other. Atet is very talented. Khemit was teaching her some of her special weaves."

"Who is this man, and when did she meet him?"

"He is Ineni, a flax farmer. One of our suppliers. They met

some time after you placed Atet with us. One look at each other, and..." She shrugged.

"Sometimes it happens like that." Apollodorus said, and both women jumped at the sound of his voice.

Tarset recovered first and inclined her head in acknowledgement. "Sometimes it does. She told us they waited only on the next crop, and then suddenly Ineni came to her and said he had received a rich gift from a patron and they didn't have to wait any longer. So we fetched a priest and had the wedding here."

"Who was this patron?"

"Ineni didn't call him by name. I'm not sure Atet knew it."

"Do you know where Ineni lives?"

Tarset's brow creased. "Not far. It wasn't as if he was taking her to some backwards little village upriver. Busirus? I could ask the other women."

"Would you, please? And send me word if you have any from Atet. I would like to see her again."

Tarset left them and Tetisheri and Apollodorus looked under and inside and behind everything in the loft once more, and found nothing that hinted at what Khemit might have discovered in the short time she had had left to her to investigate the theft of the new coins.

And nothing at all to hint at the role she played for the queen.

But when they left, Tetisheri had Apollodorus bundle up the unfinished weaving from the lap loom and stow it in his satchel.

"And who is Atet?" Apollodorus said once they were back out on the street.

"A girl from upriver."

"One of your rescuees?"

"Yes. She was skilled in weaving, so I placed her with Khemit."

"And you want to talk to her because…"

"She may remember something Tarset doesn't, and she will talk more freely to me than to Tarset or any of the other women."

"Their grief seems genuine."

They had left behind a room full of women weeping in each other's arms, none of whom had been able to confirm the name of Ineni's village. "I don't doubt their grief, but they were loyal to Khemit and will be doubly so now. If she had any secrets they won't tell them to me."

"You think this dissatisfied customer, if that is what he was, has anything to do with Khemit's murder?"

"I don't know," she said, "but I'll know more after I talk to Atet."

The sun was sinking rapidly into the west, casting long shadows along the Way. Vendors were closing up their carts and shops, looking pleased or not as the case might be at the end of the day's business, and ready to discuss the latest rumors from abroad over a cup of wine at their favorite taverna. Housewives scurried home followed by slaves laden with bags and bundles and boxes. Scholars with that ever so slightly panicked expression of those who had lately been challenged by the radical concept of critical thinking walked smack into anyone who didn't get out of their way first, although through long practice Alexandrians were adept at doing so.

"I'm hungry and my feet hurt," Apollodorus said. "I have to check in at the gymnasium, and then I'll buy you dinner."

Tetisheri's stomach reminded her that she hadn't eaten since snacking with the queen herself, and there was no one else with whom she could discuss the events of the day, which she wanted desperately to do. "All right," she said.

"Good."

He smiled down at her, and her idiot heart skipped a beat.

The Five Soldiers was located near the Palestra, on a side street across the Canopic Way from the Great Library and the Museum. It was a solidly built, single story building made of stone, with a double wooden door located in the center of the wall facing the street. A frieze of open cutouts in a repeating Greek key design lined the walls beneath the eaves, the doors were unadorned, and the only sign of what business the building might be housing were two life-size bronze statues on marble plinths: one of a man crouched over the beginning of a discus throw and the other of a man in the act of hurling a javelin.

"These are new," Tetisheri said.

Apollodorus spared them a glance. "Yes, just last month. We were replacing some of our equipment and Isidoros convinced the rest of us that we needed to dress up the outside."

"They aren't overdone like so much of that old Greek statuary you see in the Museum."

"Yes, all thick necks and improbable muscles. Dub said if Isidoros insisted on tarting up the place that the tarts had to look like real people."

Tetisheri laughed. Dubnorix, one of Apollodorus' partners in the Five Soldiers, was Alemanni and never held back on an opinion, but then ex-soldiers were not famed for their tact, especially those ex-members of the Roman Army who weren't Roman.

The door opened as they came up to it and a group of Egyptian boys tumbled through, sweaty and laughing and shoving and nudging each other in an excess of high spirits. They saw Apollodorus and came to an abrupt halt. "Good evening, sir," they said, almost in chorus.

He gave them an amiable nod. "Good practice?"

"Very good, sir!"

"Excellent." Apollodorus smiled. "Now go home and tell your parents so they'll keep paying our outrageous fees."

The boys blushed and laughed and lingered, hoping for more from the great man, but he stood back to let Tetisheri precede him into the building, nodded goodbye, and closed the door firmly. A sudden increase in chatter and laughter tapered off as the boys moved off down the street.

"Do you teach boys that age yourself?"

"I take the advanced students."

She came to a sudden halt. He stopped, too, and looked at her, brow raised. "What?"

She said, almost accusingly, "You're not the queen's bodyguard anymore, are you?"

He considered his reply. "She has other uses for me now."

"Since when?" When he didn't answer she said, "You are hiding something from me, Apollodorus."

He smiled down at her. "Many, many things, Tetisheri."

Before she could respond shouts went up from all over the room.

"Cat!"

"Ho, the little Cat is back!"

"Tetisheri, my beautiful little maiden of the Nile!"

A man who looked like Silenus minus the hooves and horns trotted over to sweep up Tetisheri in his arms and swing her around. "It has been so long I almost don't recognize you! Did you forget the way here? Alexandria is not so big a town as that. For shame!"

He was elbowed to one side by a second man who looked like an Alemanni Hercules. He had red hair and blue eyes and a long face that was sad only in repose. He flicked her nose and grinned down at her, even farther down than Apollodorus had to. "You have been away from us too long, Tetisheri, but I am too glad to see you to be angry with you."

A man who could have been his twin flipped her Bast pendant so it hit her nose and laughed at her protest. "Our

Cat always comes home, Castus, you know that." He fixed her with a stern eye. "Have you been keeping up your practice, Tetisheri?"

"Of course she has, Crixus, you can tell by the way she moves." A fourth man strolled up, matching Apollodorus in height but dark of hair and eye with swarthy skin. They all looked like the veterans they were but Dubnorix looked as if he'd retired from the front lines to a soiree with the Nomarch of Ka-K'am, with an expensive stop at his tailor's along the way.

Dub, Crixus and Castus looked to be the same age as Apollodorus while Is was older by ten or even twenty years. As with Apollodorus it was difficult to tell his true age. All five bore scars that told of front line service under arms and they carried themselves with the same easy confidence she had seen once already that day in Caesar's man Cotta, moving with the same swagger that was almost but not quite arrogance. Called upon to serve they would offer discipline, focus, intelligence and ability.

But, as she looked around the beaming circle, not necessarily allegiance. They were their own men. Even Apollodorus, she realized with a slight sense of shock, the queen's longest serving staff member to date, would choose to whom he bowed his head.

It was as if accepting the queen's commission had opened her eyes where once they had been closed, at least to the true nature of these five men, all of whom had been a part of her life since she was ten years old.

Before she could come to terms with this new awareness Dub took her hand in both of his and smiled into her eyes. "Ignore these ruffians and come away with me to Santorin. I'll take up farming and we will feed on cheese made from the milk of our own goats and on olives grown on our own trees, and we will watch the sun set on the Middle Sea as we drink of wine made from our own grapes." He kissed her hand.

Apollodorus looked at the ceiling and sighed as the rest of them dissolved into hoots and catcalls. "I'd buy your passage just to see if you could bear to get your dainty hands dirty," Isidoros said with a grunt of laughter.

Dub winked at Tetisheri and released her hand, saying with lofty scorn, "I meant, of course, a gentleman farmer."

Tetisheri laughed, her slight unease vanishing. "I see that during my allegedly long absence nothing has changed."

Nothing had. The room was still high and square and open. One corner was covered with mats devoted to practicing pankration and wrestling. A boxing ring stood next to an armory featuring every hand-held weapon from the Roman gladius and the Thracian sica to the pilum, the peltast, and the Scythian bow. The central area was strewn with more mats for individual training and, as Tetisheri well knew, an area outside as large as the interior was reserved for group tactics and target shooting.

All four walls were hung with shields featuring the insignia of armies from every nation touching the Middle Sea and more from the north, some very old and probably very valuable. Some were made of wood, some of boiled leather, some were reinforced with crossed strips of metal. Some were round, some were oval, one was an elongated rectangle made of bronze almost green with age. Pride of place was taken by a Thracian double cutout with brass studs ringing a double-headed eagle. There were dents beneath the many applications of polish, but then none of the shields looked as if they had been made merely for show.

Between the shields and the windows was a border of illustrations depicting every Olympic event since Coroibos won the first footrace and featuring male figures whose bodies were so obscenely well muscled their heads and penises looked tiny by comparison. "That's new."

Apollodorus followed her gaze and sighed. "Yes."

"Isidoros again?"

"Dub, alas, was out of town at the time."

She bit down on her lower lip, hard, to remind herself that Is was still in the room and would be mortally offended if she burst out laughing. "Pity."

"As you say." He raised his voice. "Any problems, boys?"

Crixus barred the main door as Castus and Isidoros made neat piles of the mats and slung used towels into large baskets. "None," Dub said, observing all this activity with a critical eye. "Membership is up significantly over last year, though." Crixus moved to help Is and Castus stack weapons. "The new recruits to the Queen's Guard, the more serious ones at any rate, are showing up in large numbers. That subsidy the queen gave them for extra coaching, well—"

He rubbed his nose and grinned. "Much of it is finding its way into our pockets, bless her."

"Remind me to send her a fruit basket," Apollodorus said.

"And we've had a smaller influx of young Romans, as well, although I expect that number to drop once Caesar departs." The other three men finished their tidying up and Dub dusted his hands together in approval. "The rest of us were talking over the possibility of an evening session, twice, even three times a week."

Apollodorus considered. "We'd have to increase the staff."

"We're going to have to do that anyway," Crixus said.

Castus nodded. "We made our reputation on individual attention to each member."

"It's why they come here babes crying for their mommas and leave fighters," Is said in a satisfied manner.

"Do we foresee any... problems between the different groups?"

"The Greeks and Egyptians seem to get along well enough," Dub said.

"Which only means they save the drubbings they give one another for somewhere off site," Isidoros said. "But I doubt that mixing in a few Romans is going to make the sweat smell any differently when they're all working out together."

"If there were problems, we could segregate the different groups on different nights," Dub said. "Even the days." He winked at Tetisheri. "The way we do the women students."

Apollodorus shook his head. "Our charter specifically states that we are open to all citizens, all states. Let's not draw the attention of some nosy scribe at the Palace who makes his living from imposing civil fines."

The other four men nodded. "And open nights?" Dub said.

"Let's try one and see how fast it fills up. Do any of you have people in mind to fill out the staff?"

All four men nodded again.

"I might have a name or two myself. Good. Anything else?"

"Renni the Egyptian—you remember him, short, late twenties, beard like he lets the rats gnaw on it every night, enough energy to row every boat in Caesar's fleet from here to Rome and back again? Renni dropped by this morning with a proposition."

"He wants to rent the front of the building to open a taverna!" Isidoros said.

"You're just thrilled at the prospect of not having to walk farther than the front door for your first beer," Crixus said.

"Not a taverna, Is, no wine and only small beer. Mostly juices, he says, and healthy snacks like yogurt and fruit and cheese, all fresh from the pomegranate or goat, respectively, designed to appeal to the man who has just sweated out half his body weight in our gymnasium."

"And maybe wants to brag to his friends how he took down one of us in the ring."

"Which would be a lie because no one ever has," Isidoros said.

"True." Dub looked at Apollodorus. "What do you think?"

"What kind of split is he offering?"

"Split? He said straight rent."

Apollodorus shook his head. "Offer him a sixty-forty split, we get the forty. Let him bargain you down to seventy-thirty. If we're partners, we have a say in what he sells, and to whom. And tell him Wozer keeps the books and divvies the take or no deal. Agreed?" He looked around the circle. "Good. All right, I'm off."

Dub smiled at Tetisheri. "May we come, too?"

"No, you may not," Apollodorus said.

Dub winked again at Tetisheri who was, infuriatingly, blushing again. "Great, thanks, we'd love to join you."

And so they were a group of six as they exited through the small door at the back, just as the cleaning crew of freed-women was coming in laden with mops and brooms and cloths. Apollodorus paused as the door closed behind them. "If we start night sessions, we'll have to work out something with Heret. If they have to come later to clean, we'll have to provide an escort to and from their homes."

Every hand went up. Apollodorus rolled his eyes.

They walked west, laughing and chattering, the sunset casting long shadows from the columns and fountains that lined the Way. After they passed the promenade and crossed beneath the Central Aqueduct (attempts to name it for Ptolemy XII had failed utterly, as had all attempts to name it for every Ptolemy ruler since Ptolemy I), Apollodorus led the way down a side street. There they found a small taverna tucked into an alley with an unusually benevolent Dionysus over the door, clearly inviting them in for dinner, if not for debauchery. It looked less than prepossessing from the outside but once inside revealed itself to be cozy and clean and well lit by lamps that didn't smoke, and if the scents that tickled the nose were any indication boasted a cook who knew his or her business. There were few empty tables, which also boded well, and no Romans, which was even better. Once the Romans did inevitably discover the place the prices would go up and available tables would become nonexistent.

"Apollodorus! Come in, come in! And you brought friends! Splendid!" A large woman bustled forward. Her face was round and flushed, her luxuriant dark hair caught up in a careless knot of curls. She was tying a fresh apron over a floor-length gray tunic that was well-worn but clean. It was sleeveless and her arms bulged with muscles developed, one imagined, over years of heaving heavy pots about.

"Edeva! Well met." They clasped hands and Apollodorus leaned forward to give her a noisy kiss on the cheek. Edeva flushed even darker, laughed and swatted at him, and then at the other four men who kissed her in turn. Afterward, her cheeks redder than ever, she looked at Tetisheri with interest. "And who do we have here?"

"A friend."

She raised her eyebrows. "Oh ho, like that, is it? Sit, sit." She waved them to a round table in the corner that had miraculously emptied as they walked in. "You're just in time for the last servings of tonight's special. I'll send the girl out with wine. Sit!"

They sat as she bustled into another room.

"I like this place," Tetisheri said. "Who is Edeva?"

"She is from far to the north," Dub said.

"From a large island known for druids," Crixus said.

"And warrior queens," Is said, waggling his eyebrows and his tongue, for which he was promptly elbowed by both Crixus and Castus.

"And fighters who paint themselves blue," Castus said. "For the gods alone know what reason."

"Britannia?" Tetisheri said.

"You've heard of it?"

She shrugged. "I've read Caesar's memoir."

"There's a copy in the Library?"

"In Greek?"

"There are many," Tetisheri said dryly, "in any language you choose. Our queen saw to that before he ever arrived. There was something of a last-minute rush on the various translations. Crispinus was… eloquent on the subject."

"Ah," Dub said. "Yes, of course. His own name is undoubtedly the first thing Caesar would have looked for in the Great Library."

The girl arrived with a pitcher of wine that Dub deemed palatable, and everyone settled in over their cups with a palpable sigh of relaxation.

"To be fair," Tetisheri said, "he's a better writer than most."

"To hear him tell it, Caesar is an entire legion unto himself."

"He certainly goes through women as if he were," Is said,

and the conversation took a turn for the bawdy at Caesar's expense, including a verse declaimed by Crixus with the utmost severity and joined in in full voice by Dub, Is and Castus on the last line.

Home we bring our bald whoremonger
Romans, lock your wives away!
All the bags of gold you lent him
Went his Gallic tarts to pay.

Everyone else in the taverna from patron to cook laughed and applauded. Tetisheri laughed, too, but she also cast a quick glance around the room. "Good thing there aren't any Romans present. They might take exception."

"My poor sweet innocent," Dub said, grinning, "who do you think we learned it from?"

Is couldn't contain himself. "It's every Roman legion's favorite marching song! Caesar himself has probably sung along to it!"

She looked at Apollodorus for confirmation.

"Never mind expecting a laugh out of him at a rude poem," Dub said, "he's by far too big a prude."

Apollodorus pretended not to hear, and under cover of dinner arriving Isidoros whispered earnestly, "He isn't really, Sheri."

"It wasn't exactly an insult, Is," she said, but indulged her curiosity anyway. "He doesn't—well, he doesn't visit Joy Street?"

Is shook his head. "It's not his way."

He rubbed the back of his hand where a crust was forming over a new wound. She nodded at it. "What happened?"

The impish satyr grinned. "A moment of carelessness." He looked past her at Apollodorus. "I should know better than to test that one on the net and trident. He is definitely his father's son."

This was more than Is had ever said about the Five Soldiers' lives before they came to Alexandria and Tetisheri said, as indifferently as she could manage, "Indeed? His father was a retiarius, then?"

"The best who ever raised a trident or threw a net," he said. He gave her a shrewd look that told her she hadn't sounded as indifferent as she might have wished. "All of our fathers spilled blood on the sands of the arena."

"I thought the five of you came to Alexandria with Antony's cavalry."

"We did, but that was after."

"Why the change of profession?" She tried to say it lightly but his somber expression forbade humor.

"To be a soldier is one thing. To kill other men, brothers they came to be, equally skilled at arms, for no reason other than the entertainment of an arena full of Romans screaming for blood? It didn't matter whose." He shook his head. "I didn't want that for the boys, and their fathers definitely wouldn't have wanted it, either."

"Their fathers?" she said, startled.

He let out a bray of laughter. "Oh no, no, no, Sheri, you

dear sweet girl, I was never that ambitious. I stand as father figure to them all, yes, in all but blood."

"Then how—"

He gave her an odd look. "Shall we say their fathers commended them to my care, and leave it at that?"

Edeva interrupted further confidences with an enormous bowl of seasoned lamb stew plonked down in the center of the table, and surrounded it with a pile of fresh baked bread, and conversation died. A refill of the stew came before it was called for, along with a resupply of the bread and wine. Edeva was familiar with these particular customers, it seemed. At any rate, they ate heartily and swabbed up the last of the gravy with the last chunks of bread. The serving girl brought a bowl of grapes and Edeva followed her with an assortment of cheeses on a platter and another pitcher, this time of chilled fruit juice. There were no complaints, and Tetisheri realized that in all the years she had known the Five Soldiers, she had never seen any one of them the worse for drink. Something else she'd never noticed. She wasn't entirely sure she was comfortable with this newly revealed ability to see what had not been seen before. It was almost as if she had grown another eye.

Crixus belched and shoved back from the table. Since Castus shared his bench he perforce moved back with him. Crixus overrode his protest and gathered up Dub and Is as well, which would have been fine if he hadn't winked at Apollodorus on his way out.

Apollodorus selected a grape. "Shall we run through the

evidence gathered thus far?" She raised her eyes and found him looking at her with a steady gaze, expression bland, to all appearances totally unconscious of the not so subtle meaning of Crixus' wink.

She cleared her throat and sipped at her juice. "Very well," she said, and raised her eyes, determined to maintain her composure even as he stared so. "Someone other than you, the queen, Sosigenes, and Captain Laogonus knew of the shipment, and all of its details. The theft was far too well planned to be otherwise."

"You rule out Laogonus as a suspect, then?"

She shook her head. "I don't, but you obviously do, which means the queen does as well. I want to get this—this task done and over with as soon as possible, and I prefer not to waste my time investigating a suspect who doesn't exist."

He popped a chunk of hard cheese in his mouth, and chewed ruminatively. "Someone in the palace, do you think?"

"Or someone in Lemesos. Or one of the deckhands. Oh, I know what the good captain said, that his crew has been with him forever, but anyone can be tempted by enough coin."

"As this surely is," he said, his mouth grim. "Even so small a share as he would be offered, it would be enough."

"Where are the deckhands?"

His eyes widened in mock innocence. "You heard Laogonus. On leave." She snorted, and he smiled. "All right. They are under guard in a house near the Palace."

"We will go there and question them following our meal."

"We will go there and question them tomorrow morning," he said firmly. "What of Khemit?"

"Khemit," she said, leaning back against the wall. "I find it interesting that Khemit was killed not two full days after she had an altercation with a customer in her own shop, and most especially that the employee who saw him most nearly was fortuitously dowered and whisked out of the city the very next day."

She looked around the room again and dropped her voice. "But I also find it almost too much to believe that someone entrusted with the Eye of Isis could be so maladroit as to allow a suspect to follow her home."

"Still," he said.

She sighed. "Still. I would like to know who that gentleman was, and why he was so upset that day."

"Possibly, no matter what Tarset says about the perfect satisfaction Khemit's business delivers, he was in fact there to complain of the quality of the length of linen he had bought there."

She smiled faintly. "Possibly."

"But not likely," he said. "And we are no closer to finding who stole the new issue right out from under the queen's nose, or where it is now. Thebes, probably. If not Meroe."

"Oh no, the coin is still here in Alexandria."

He sat back and regarded her with a quizzical expression. "You seem very certain."

"It's heavy, which makes it hard to move. It's new, which

makes it impossible to spend. And the best place to spend it will be a large port, where its newness will be at least somewhat less obvious mixed in with all the other coins from around the Middle Sea. Oh no, the new coins are still here in the city." She looked around the room, which had emptied out while they were eating. "And I'm not altogether certain that this was a theft motivated by greed."

He raised an eyebrow. "What else would such a theft be motivated by?"

She reached into her purse, pulling out a handful of money and spreading it on the table. Coins of various denominations and nationalities stared up at them. The largest was of bronze, and Apollodorus touched it with a fingertip. "He's a long way from home. That's Saladas I. I was born in the third year of his reign." He turned it over. "And look, on the other side, the double-headed eagle of Thrace."

The smallest was also bronze, a lepton from Judea. Other coins of bronze and a few silver ranged in size in between the first two. "Uncle Neb just got back from upriver," Tetisheri said. "He said it was getting harder to buy anything outright for the lack of coin in hand, that he was having to resort to barter. While he was gone, I, too, noticed there is more Roman silver than Egyptian bronze in circulation." She remembered what the queen had said that morning. "Fewer coins in circulation increases the value of those coins still in circulation, giving them a higher value than what shows on the face of the coin. People naturally turn to more and smaller coins of lesser value, like Greek stater or—"

"Roman denarii?"

"Or Roman denarii. Or even gold. You won't believe it, but last week someone paid with a Persian daric. It had an image of a crowned lion eating a bull." She reflected for a moment. "Or mating with him, I couldn't tell for sure." When he shouted with laughter she said defensively, "Yes, but it was an old coin, Apollodorus, and the surface worn near smooth."

"Old coins can be very valuable," he said, still chuckling. "People collect them, and often pay well over their face value to acquire them."

She gave him a reproving look. "I am aware. I have it safe for Uncle Neb to deal with. He has several acquaintances who have him watch for such rarities as come through our hands." She paused. "It was very old, Apollodorus, perhaps from the time of Alexander himself. Who knows, it may have passed through his very hands."

"Be careful or you'll be starting your own coin collection before long."

She laughed. "No chance of that. I'm much more interested in coins being used for what they are made for, changing hands for goods and services. Much more fun than putting one on display to be admired."

"Mmmm."

"What?"

"The coins were made in Cyprus."

"And?"

"And... should you perhaps go there?"

This was something she had not considered in the course of the investigation thus far. She did so now. "I won't rule it out," she said at last, "but it seems to no purpose."

"And why is that?"

She shrugged. "The coin was stolen in Alexandria, not in Cyprus. Remember Laogonus said he knew it was valuable because it was heavy."

"Those chests could have been loaded with rocks for all Laogonus knew."

"Perhaps," she said. "And certainly, information about the shipment could have been sold as easily from Lemesos as from Alexandria." She thought for a moment. "If the shipment is not quickly found, then, yes, I suppose a trip to Cyprus might be in order."

He scooped up her coins and handed them to her, and then tossed a handful of his own on the table—only one of them with an image of a Ptolemaic king, she noted—and rose to his feet. "Edeva! We're going!"

The big woman came bustling out from behind the partition and examined the cleaned plates with evident satisfaction. "Well, and it is always nice to see customers enjoying their food."

"I would guess it is impossible not to enjoy a meal at Edeva's," Tetisheri said.

Edeva beamed. "You can bring this one back anytime, Apollodorus."

He smiled at Tetisheri again, who, to her continuing annoyance, blushed again. It was becoming chronic. Perhaps

Zotikos had a salve. Although if he couldn't even make a potion to ease menstrual cramps he probably wasn't the best person to ask.

"You can count on it, Edeva," Apollodorus said. Oh yes, he'd noticed the blush.

Edeva escorted them to the door where they made their farewells and stepped outside. Behind them, a bar dropped into brackets. Before them, the moon was only just rising and even though it was on the wane the light it shed was enough to turn Alexandria into a city of ghosts and shadows, pristine white pillars that the moonlight turned almost translucent, dark lines cast by the corniced roofs of massive buildings set back from the Way, and the Way itself, that broad thorough-fare so crowded during the day. Now, of course, the Way was quiet, or mostly so, most of her citizens home for the night but for those patronizing the few tavernas granted by royal charter (and in exchange for the appropriate fee) permission to stay open until the Eighteenth Hour, when Aristander's night watch would see to it that their shutters were put firmly up on the hour. Even the camp of the Queen's Guard was blessedly quiet, the new recruits nursing their self-inflicted wounds in their tents and the sergeants in theirs planning new tortures for the morrow.

"What are your plans for tomorrow?"

"I want to talk to Laogonus' crew," she said. "And I want to see where Khemit died."

He paused. "Should I have taken you to see it? On my word nothing was found but what you saw."

"I should like to see it all the same."

"Aristander will show you if I don't get back in time."

"And I will make a summary of what we have discovered thus far," she said. "It would be best if we kept a record of everything we discover. Where are you going?"

"I will ride out to Busirus," he said. "To see if I can find this flax farmer and his new bride."

"You think it's that important?"

"It doesn't matter what I think," he said, parroting her earlier words about Laogonus. "You do, and you're the one in charge of this investigation."

Tetisheri was not lacking in confidence—hard won, in her case, over a difficult childhood and an even more difficult marriage, however brief—but still she was a little taken aback, and found herself at an unaccustomed lack for words. They walked west toward where Tetisheri would turn north toward the docks and home. They paused at the intersection of the streets. She looked up at him, his fair hair turned to silver threads by Sefkhet's fine hand. His expression as he looked upon her was hard to read. "Thank you for your escort today, Apollodorus. I accomplished much more than I would have otherwise. Especially since I have no idea what I'm doing."

She thought she saw the trace of a smile cross his face. "You did fine."

She started to contradict him when he caught her hand in his and kissed it. His lips were firmer and warmer than Deb's, and they lingered a lot longer on her skin. Her heart seemed simply to stop beating in that moment. When he turned her hand in his own to kiss her palm, it started beating again, hard and fast, a positive thunder in her ears. She knew everything she felt was revealed on her face in that moment.

He bowed his head and left without a word. She stared after him, her mouth slightly open, her breath coming fast.

Which may have been why she paid less attention than she might have while negotiating those few blocks left to her own front door. As she reached for the latch she became belatedly aware of the sound of footsteps behind her. A smothering darkness fell over her head.

She screamed, and something struck her temple. Stunned, she was conscious only of being lifted off her feet and carried away.

5

on the evening of the Tenth Day of the Second Week
at the Fifteenth Hour...

She did not lose consciousness but her head was swimming from the blow and she was gasping for air that wasn't there. She seemed to be enveloped in a coarse blanket of some kind. One set of arms was wrapped tightly around her torso, which didn't help with her breathing, the other around her knees, and if the way she was being jarred and jolted was any indication they were running. Until she could breathe and see to fight there was no point in fighting, so she clenched her teeth and tried to keep some track of their route. They made few turns or so it seemed to her, keeping to a straight path. West from her doorstep would lead to the Port of Eunostos. Was she to be put aboard a ship? East would have them passing through the heart of the city, the Amphitheater, the public baths, the Queen's Guard's training camp, the...

The Royal Palace.

Her captors never spoke a word to each other. Men, they had to be, and disciplined to keep silence. Soldiers? A personal guard? Trained, certainly. Employed by whom?

They jolted to a stop, a hard knock on wood, a door creaked open, and they moved forward again, their footsteps louder now that they were inside. A pause, a muffled challenge, another door, footsteps on a hard surface. Then she was on her feet, the blanket covering her ripped off and she was being forced to her knees and her head to the floor. She was happy enough there for the moment, concentrating on catching her breath and getting her heart rate under control.

No one called her name or demanded she rise so she took in as much of the room as she could from her cramped position. It was large and brilliantly lit by so many candles that it took a moment for her eyes to accustom themselves to the light. She dared a glance to either side and saw many pairs of feet, a few female, more male, all of them wearing slippers and sandals that Uncle Neb would have instantly recognized as the product of only the very best shoemakers in Alexandria. One pair seemed to be made of gold, another of silver, a third of leather cleverly gilded with what appeared to be both. One of the men wore a pair made entirely of cabochons of carnelian fastened together with copper links that looked oddly familiar.

There were furniture feet, too, elaborately carved in the shapes of animals. There was one very realistic crocodile that seemed to be staring right at her. His teeth were even painted white. Or possibly inlaid with mother of pearl. The floor was polished marble and what she could see of the walls seemed to be plaster painted wet with figures from Greek myths in every color of the rainbow; Zeus, Hera, Aphrodite tempting Hephaestus, Athena with her shield, Mercury with his winged sandals, Poseidon with his trident.

She was very much afraid she knew exactly where she was.

"Well, get her up on her feet," a pettish voice said. "We can't question her with her face on the floor."

"And we can always put her back there," someone else said with a snigger. "On her back, preferably."

The first voice laughed, a high-pitched nasal sound. "Indeed we can, Naevius, and we will."

A hand fastened in her hair and yanked her up. She gritted her teeth and did not, would not cry out. If these were her last moments in this world she would not give her kidnappers the satisfaction of showing one iota of fear.

Ptolemy XIV Theos Philopator II sat in a gilt chair so large his head barely topped its overly ornate arms. His feet would have dangled well above the floor if someone hadn't first placed them tenderly on a golden footstool carved in the shape of a hippopotamus. "Ah," he said, twisting his lips into what he obviously believed was a sneer meant to demonstrate how far above her he was. "The half-breed friend of my mongrel sister. How nice of you to join us." He affected a yawn. "Why did we want to soil our air with her presence again, Philo? Linos? Anyone?"

Cleopatra's co-ruler was a pudgy adolescent with small muddy brown eyes set unnaturally far apart, so that he gave the impression of never meeting anyone's gaze straight on. His lips were thick and pursed in a permanent pout. His hair was sparse and he had made a pitiful attempt to comb it forward in the style of Caesar. Thick eye paint extended into points that reached his temples, his cheeks were rouged, his lips and nails were painted gold, and he was clad in a pleated cloth of gold shenti that wrapped him like a mummy from the waist down, leaving the hairless concavity of his chest exposed. The heavy gold uraeus on his brow sat a little off-center, which seemed somehow appropriate.

Here, Tetisheri thought, here before her sat the product of three centuries of inbreeding, of brother marrying sister and producing progeny that became steadily more unbalanced with every generation. No wonder the Flute Player had gone looking for new blood to invigorate the line of the Ptolemies.

His stare was oddly incurious for someone who had evidently ordered her kidnapping and he seemed in no hurry for her to speak so she looked around the room. If her life in this world was to be so disastrously shortened, she might as well identify the eyewitnesses so she could give their names to Bast on her journey to the next one. Her hand crept up to the pendant hanging from her neck and closed on it convulsively. She straightened her shoulders and raised her chin, at the same time identifying all available exits and impediments between them and her, estimating the level of resistance she would meet if she tried to flee, calculating what her odds were if she decided to fight. Whatever they were, she would die fighting before she let them lay hands on her and she would do her very best to take some of them with her. Crixus would be so proud.

It appeared she had interrupted the royal dinner, now coming to its end. There were slaves offering trays of fruit and cheese and honey-glazed pastries to the guests sitting or lying on couches arrayed around the king in two arcs. She herself stood in the space where their ends almost met. There was usually some small entertainment at the end of these affairs and tonight she appeared to be it. How nice.

"The peel is still on this apple," Ptolemy said, and slapped away the tray proffered by a slave. The contents went everywhere and the tray skittered across the floor to come to rest a hand's width from Tetisheri's left foot. It was enough like a discus that it would do for a projectile at need. "Have him flogged, Linos. I want his back bleeding when next I see him."

The slave, a boy of twelve, burst into tears and fell to his knees, and was dragged off by one of the guards. The company barely noticed.

She might even be able to remove the little monster's head from his shoulders before they got to her.

To the right of the king sat three Romans, one older, the other two younger. The elder looked familiar and after a moment she recognized him. He was one of the two who had come into the queen's presence with Caesar. Not Cotta but the long-faced one, who had looked at the queen with such intent. The two youths with him looked enough like him for her to identify them as his sons. His nose was elevated and his displeasure manifest, which might have had something to do with the honey-roasted fig that had landed in his lap during the king's temper tantrum.

To the left of the king was a small group of his advisors. There was Linos the Eunuch, the king's political advisor. He wore bright blue silk and dark kohl and red carnelian on neck, arms, and feet. Philo was an Alexandrian aristocrat of such high lineage he made Tetisheri's former mother-in-law look like a liberal, and was head of the faction of nobles that supported Ptolemy and hated Ptolemy's sister on principal.

General Thales, known as the new Theodotos, stood at parade rest with his hands clasped behind his back, dressed in a simple linen tunic with a leather belt, wrist guards and sandals, and no jewelry whatever. He had a square, rugged face, currently looking as if it had been used as a model for a tomb carving in Memphis. His expression didn't change when their eyes met and she made sure that neither did hers, but she did breathe a little easier when she saw him.

The man standing a little apart from the first three she did not know. He looked Greek and dressed like an Egyptian. His skin seldom saw the sun and his arms and legs were so long he looked like a white, four-legged spider standing upright. His eyes were close set and dark and pitiless and from between them a long, beaked nose protruded like the corvus on a Roman quinquireme.

Next to the group of counselors Tetisheri recognized

Nenwef, sharing a couch with a woman who was definitely not his wife.

There was one lone Egyptian present. This was a lovely little girl of seven or eight with blue-black skin, a broad nose, wide, flat cheekbones, full lips and a soft cloud of hair that fell down to her waist. She wore a gold collar and nothing else. To the collar was attached a leash, the other end of which was held by the Alexandrian sitting to the Romans' right. This was Lord Hunefer, Nomarch of Marimda, companion and advisor to Ptolemy XIV, and Tetisheri's former husband.

Next to Hunefer was, of course, his mother, Ipwet. A thin woman carrying her weight in heavy gold bracelets and a collar that covered her shoulders, she wore her hair cut straight across her brow in the fashion of the ancient Pharaohs. Which in other circumstances Tetisheri might have found hilarious, since Ipwet claimed to be a descendant of Ptolemy I. Not close enough in blood to be a threat to the current co-rulers, goodness me, no, Ipwet wasn't that foolish, but not so distant as to not be able to offer up a convincing whiff of royal privilege whenever it came time to pay her bills or her taxes. Not so convincing with Cleopatra in power. It was no surprise to see Ipwet and her son in Ptolemy's train.

Ipwet pretended not to see Tetisheri. Tetisheri pretended not to see her right back. Whatever she could expect from her ex-mother-in-law, help was not it.

The rest in attendance were minor Alexandrian nobles accompanied by wives or one of Caesar's ex-tarts. Most of them looked as if they had spent a long evening being bored by Ptolemy Theos' determination to focus all attention on himself and were now looking at her as a relief.

She herself had yet to speak and she was determined not to unless she was spoken to first. The king was pleased to scowl. She could only hope she would continue to disappoint him.

"Well?" the king said. "What were you conspiring at this afternoon with that black bitch dressed up like Pharaoh? Tell me and I may yet let you live." He looked at Linos and Philo. "Is that not generous of me? To make such an offer to a traitor to Alexandria and Egypt? Am I not the kindest and most merciful of all the kings ever to sit on the throne of Egypt?"

His voice was high and piercing. Theirs were low and deferential.

"The most kind, O king."

"Wisest and most merciful, Ptolemy Theos, Fourteenth of His Name, there is no doubt."

"The most cunning and courageous ever to wear the Double Crown."

A concurring murmur ran around the room.

Tetisheri found a bas-relief carving in the molding that lined the walls of the room below the roof and above the wall paintings and studied it. Theseus and the Minotaur, perhaps. Or the rape of Europa, if the sculptor had been far-sighted. Or a misogynist.

"Speak!" the king said sharply. "What was so important that forced that stinking cunt out of Caesar's bed?"

She knew full well she was about to die. Nothing she said would change that outcome, so she stiffened her spine and remained silent.

The king's face darkened and she couldn't help it, she ducked away from the blow she knew was coming from one or both of the guards standing behind her. It fell on her shoulder and almost knocked her off her feet. She caught herself before she fell, straightened her shoulders and went back to studying the molding illustrations. All Greek, of course. No Egyptian gods need apply. Where did this overprivileged brat imagine all his wealth came from? It was something he had never learned and that his sister never forgot.

A second blow fell across her shoulders, another almost immediately on her back, and then the blows rained thick and fast, catching her shoulders and arms and the sides of her head. Her sight blurred, her ears rang, she tried dropping to the floor and curling into a ball but two more guards came to grasp her by the hands and pull her to her feet, there to hold her so the first two could continue beating her.

Something that sounded suspiciously like a stamp came from the throne. "Who does this bint think she is! Linos! Tell them to break out the whips! Make her speak! She is not allowed to ignore me! I am her king!"

There was the sound of a throat clearing. "My king—" Thales, that was. "Perhaps—"

The blows slowed and Tetisheri began to shift her weight to her right foot as she pulled her arms in and clenched her fists, moving back as she turned to strike. And then the tray, she thought, bringing her left hand up to guard, her right to strike.

Outside the doors was a clang and a thud, followed by another clang and another thud. There was a low moan. The attention of the room shifted from the disappointing lack of drama in front of them—another slave being beaten, what could be more dull—to the door, which swung invitingly wide. The hard hands grasping Tetisheri's wrists loosened and fell away. She managed to remain upright, although she was dizzy and nauseous and her shoulders and back ached fiercely.

Apollodorus strolled in. No, that wasn't quite accurate, Tetisheri thought. He sauntered.

Idiot! For a moment she was afraid she had said it out loud. What was he doing here? He would only get them both killed.

At the same time something in his air of nonchalance made the tight ball of fear in her abdomen ease. He tossed off what might charitably have been called a salute in Ptolemy's direction and as an afterthought acknowledged being in the presence of the co-sovereign of Alexandria and Egypt with a casual, "Majesty."

He progressed unhurriedly up the long hall and came to a stop next to Tetisheri. The guards seemed to melt away in his presence. "It grows late, love," he said, sliding a familiar arm around her waist. "I thought you might need an escort home. The streets of Alexandria being what they are at night, and citizens going about their lawful business being at risk."

He looked up to cast a glimpse around the room, his smile razor-sharp. "As they so obviously are."

Tetisheri allowed herself to lean against him, and managed to pull her mouth into a trembling smile. "How thoughtful of you, my dear." Her voice was shaking and she took a deep breath to steady it. "Your timing is impeccable. It has been a tiring day, and I am ready for my bed."

He dropped a light kiss on her nose. "Then we shall adjourn there forthwith."

They might have been alone in the room for all the notice they took of anyone else in it. Tetisheri felt a fine shudder begin in her bones and only hoped it would hold off long enough for them to get safety out of this room.

Predictably, Linos and Philo spoke together in real or feigned outrage.

"O king, such insolence!"

"You have yet to question the woman, you cannot allow—"

Thales cleared his throat again, and Linos and Philo shut up.

Into the sudden silence came a laugh and Tetisheri looked around to see the two Roman youths lost in amusement at this show to which they had the very best seats. "Pity," one said. "The king did promise us a bit of fun before the evening was over. I was hoping she was it."

"Let her go mate with her crocodile," his brother said. "What can you expect from a bunch of animal worshippers?"

"She would not make it worth your while, friends, believe

me," Hunefer said, his voice disdainful. "I tried for two years." He smiled and pulled on the leash. The little girl was jerked to her feet. "Never fear. We have other toys."

The Roman boys looked at the beautiful girl on Hunefer's leash. "I suppose we can make do."

Tetisheri saw Apollodorus' eyes narrow and felt the arm around her waist tighten. "Oh, there was just one thing before we take our leave," she said, making her voice clear enough to be heard by everyone in the room. "May I?" She got her hand on the gladius at his belt before he did, barely.

For one fraught moment she thought he might refuse her. And then he pulled the sword from its sheath and offered it to her with a slight bow.

It was solid and heavy in her hand. She turned, holding her bruised and shaken frame severely straight, and walked straight at Hunefer, who squawked like a startled duck. It did not speak well for the king's guard that they did not immediately leap between the two of them but then she was moving pretty fast. One swing of the blade and the leash holding the Egyptian slave girl fell neatly into two pieces. Hunefer dropped his end with another squawk.

The girl didn't move, looking from the severed leash to Tetisheri and back again.

"Come with us," Tetisheri said, and turned before she could see if she was obeyed. She paused long enough to return Apollodorus' gladius and walked swiftly through the doors, stepping lightly over the bodies of the two men who had been standing guard in front of them. Behind her she heard a scamper of feet. Hunefer squawked again but the girl passed Apollodorus and Tetisheri like they were standing still.

Outside again on the dark street the three of them paused, the girl poised to run, and who could blame her.

"Do you speak Greek?" Tetisheri said in that language.

A pause, then a short nod.

"You can run if you like," Tetisheri said. "No one will stop you. Or you can come home with me."

"What will I have to do once we get there?" The question was laden with suspicion.

"Bathe, put on clothes, eat if you are hungry, sleep. In the morning we'll find you something to do to earn your keep."

"A slave again. Why would I do that?"

"Not a slave," Tetisheri said. "You will be paid, and you will be free to take other employment if you wish."

"Can I go home?"

"Where is home?"

The girl looked away, her chin trembling.

"How long have you been in Alexandria?"

She didn't know the answer to either question. "Come home with me for now," Tetisheri said. "You'll be safe, and warm, and fed, and you will live among other free men and women of Alexandria and Egypt. My uncle and I keep no slaves."

"Make up your mind," Apollodorus said, grasping Tetisheri's arm and urging her down the street. "As soon as the kinglet finds his balls—or his guests find them for him—he'll send his men out after us." His pace was closer to a run than a walk and his iron grip on her arm made no allowance for any injuries she had suffered that evening. After a moment, Tetisheri heard the patter of bare feet behind them.

"How did you know?" she said, the fine trembling that had begun in Ptolemy's audience hall starting to manifest itself again now that there was no need to maintain the fiction of invulnerability.

He cut down an alley. "I heard you scream." They emerged onto a street, crossed it, went down another alley that became increasingly narrow, which then opened up into a broad avenue that Tetisheri recognized as near the Palestra, two streets up from the Way. They were headed west, toward the docks, and home. "I'm sorry," he said. "I should have walked you to your door and seen you safely inside."

"It's not your fault." She attempted a laugh. It sounded pitiful even to her own ears. "Aristander would be wounded to the core if we told him his streets weren't safe."

"For those on the queen's business, evidently they aren't," he said, and she remembered that only the night before, the Eye of Isis had been murdered on those same streets. "I came as fast as I could."

"They were moving pretty fast themselves," she said, remembering that jolting trip through the streets. "They must have feared pursuit. If they'd been following us they would have known it was you." And they wouldn't have been eager to match swords with one of the Five Soldiers.

The Queen's Guard encampment, tents pitched in orderly

rows, materialized on their right. A sentry snapped to attention. "Halt, in the name of the queen!"

"Glaucio?"

"Apollodorus?" The sentry peered at them as they came closer. "You're out late."

"I'm headed for home as we speak."

By this time Glaucio had taken in Tetisheri. "Oho." He grinned and waved them on. "Have a good night!" He tensed again, looking behind them.

"She's with us," Apollodorus said, and they left Glaucio swearing and shaking his head. They turned down a side street, walked rapidly past the Thermophoriom and came at last upon the docks. Here Apollodorus kept to the middle of the street, one hand still grasping Tetisheri's arm, the other drawing his sword with a hiss of metal.

"Are they behind us?" She was breathing hard, trying not to trip over her own stumbling feet.

"I don't think so, but I'm taking no chances. How badly hurt are you?"

"Not too badly, I don't think. They were just getting started when you came. Oh, Apollodorus." Shamefully, her voice broke on his name.

His grip tightened for a moment, painfully so, and then loosened again.

They stumbled at last to a halt in front of Uncle Neb's door. Tetisheri knocked quickly, three times, and they waited, Apollodorus with his back to her, watching the street. After a wait came the sounds of the lock and the door swung open

to reveal Keren, looking rumpled and sleepy-eyed. "Sheri?
What—"

Apollodorus muscled the two of them inside. Looking over
his shoulder Tetisheri said, "You, come here."

The little slave girl shuffled inside, looking as exhausted
as Tetisheri felt but with her glare intact. She didn't trust a
one of them, no, she did not.

"Do you have a name?" Tetisheri said.

The glare, if anything, intensified. "I won't be called by
what he called me!"

"Fine, you can choose a name tomorrow. This is Keren.
Keren, this is a new friend. Please find her a sleeping shift and
a bed. We'll worry about the rest tomorrow."

Keren took this without a blink. She smiled at the girl.
"Are you hungry? Come with me, we'll see what we can find
in the kitchen."

The girl hesitated, looked at Tetisheri, and then followed
Keren into the house.

"Apollodorus—"

He sheathed his sword and turned to her and took her
in his arms, pushing her back against the wall. Her sore
shoulders made themselves felt and she gave a muffled protest. "What—"

His face was in shadow, hers in the moonlight shining
through the open door. "I was afraid I wouldn't get there in
time." Before she could stutter a refusal he kissed her and
she froze in place, eyes wide open, staring at the fans of
his eyelashes as they lay on his cheeks. Lips touched her

eyes, the corners of her mouth, the heretofore unknown and alarmingly sensitive place beneath her ear. He pulled back to look at her. "I've never been so frightened in all my life." He slid his hand up her spine to hold her head where he wanted it and leaned in again, running his tongue down the seam of her lips, and she gasped, any thought of beatings and bruises forgotten.

Her husband had never kissed her. He had raped her, though, and she knew the meaning of the length of flesh pressed against her belly. Her first thought was to resist, to fight, to free herself, to run. Her second thought was that Apollodorus' mouth was so very warm and so very coaxing. He nibbled at her lower lip and something strange happened to her knees and she sagged against him. Her head fell back on a suddenly limp neck, her eyelids fluttered closed, all the better to concentrate on the feel of his lips, and his hands, and his body. He gave something between a grunt and a groan and kneed her legs apart and settled between them, and something that she had thought long dead, murdered at the hands of her husband, roused suddenly, outrageously, over-whelmingly to life.

"*Agape mou*," his said, his voice low and tender. The words seemed to strum against her body.

She should pull away now, she thought hazily. She really should. But she could still breathe, and she wasn't bound or under threat. At some deep level she knew if she made the slightest protest he would free her at once.

She didn't, which may have been the most amazing event

in an evening made up of one continually amazing event after another.

He raised his head at last, his face still in shadow so that she couldn't see his expression. Her lips felt swollen and ever so slightly scorched, and she was shocked to see that her arms had wound themselves around his neck of their own volition. His hands slid down to her hips to hold her firmly against that hard length. His voice was deep and rough. "Are you frightened?"

She swallowed. "No," she said, stunned to know that she was telling the truth.

"Good." He kissed her again and this time she allowed herself to forget the world, to be lost in this moment. Her skin felt as if it were on fire, her heart beat so hard and so fast she was afraid it would leap from her throat. Her breasts felt full and heavy and the secret place between her legs had turned hot and liquid and wanting.

He stepped back, reaching for her hands to pull them from his neck and clasp them in his own. "We will continue this, but not now, and not here."

She swallowed, and to her own amazement, couldn't deny it.

"Why do you save them?"

Involuntarily she ran her tongue over her lips, marveling at how sensitive they felt, and he growled deep in his throat and gave her a slight shake. "Tetisheri. Why do you save them?"

"What? Who?"

"The girls. I know Uncle Neb does it because you asked

him to. I know you've been doing it since before your marriage. Why?"

Her racing heart began to slow, and she tried to summon some order to her whirling brain to form a coherent answer. "Because they have no one, and they need someone."

"Why must it be you?"

She took a deep breath and let it out slowly. "Our queen is a good queen, but even she has slaves."

He stood silently, absorbing this. "Because she won't help them, you will?"

She shrugged.

"You can't save them all."

"But I can save some."

The smile was back in his voice. "Especially if it means stealing one right out from under Hunefer's nose?"

"He had her on a leash," she said, and there was no trace of a responding smile at all in her voice.

She saw a flash of teeth. He raised one of her hands to his mouth. As he had before, he kissed it and then reversed it to kiss her palm, only this time he bit the flesh at the base of her thumb. Some sound came out of her throat that she had never heard before, and he soothed the bite with his tongue.

He dropped her hand and stepped back. "I'll send word to the queen of the king's action this evening, which will I imagine stave off any further attempts on your liberty."

Tetisheri imagined so, too. "I wonder if she'll kill him."

"We can only hope." He sighed. "No, probably not, not with Caesar still here."

"Why is Cleopatra the only one of the Flute Player's children who has even a passing acquaintance with logic?"

"The same reason his brother decided to swim the Nile in full armor, and why Arsinoë tried to take the throne while her father and sisters and brother were still living." He shrugged. "The Ptolemies bred for blood, not brains. The result of the only time they didn't is on the throne now." He turned. "I'll see you tomorrow when I get back from Busirus. Try to keep out of trouble until then."

"Apollodorus!"

"Lady, it's late and if you're not inviting me to stay I'm for my own bed and an uncomfortable night at best. Close the door behind me because this time I'm not leaving until I hear the bolt thrown with you on the other side."

And so she found herself standing inside the atrium, listening to water trickle over the fountain, rubbing the warm, throbbing spot on her palm where he'd bitten her, her whole body itchy with a kind of dissatisfaction with which she was entirely unfamiliar.

But what she found most astonishing of all, not a dissatisfaction with which she was unhappy.

No.

She found her way to her room, undressed in the dark and climbed into her bed, where Bast joined her, curling up in the angle between her neck and her shoulder to purr in her ear.

She had known Apollodorus all her adult life. She'd had a crush on him at ten, but then all the girls in class had, Cleopatra included. He was so very handsome, so courteous and well-spoken, so intelligent, and so very, very capable that one had to wonder what else that capability might extend to. Later, when she was older, sometimes during class where he was demonstrating a handhold meant to disarm or a thrust of a blade meant to disable, he would of necessity have his hands on her, and she would imagine that he looked at her in a different way than he looked at the other girls. But then, she would tell herself, probably all the girls felt the same way. She wasn't special enough to single out.

He had seemed so much more worldly, too, with so much knowledge and experience of the world beyond the shores of Alexandria. Now that she was older herself, now that she had been through so much, now that she had journeyed so far with Uncle Neb, Apollodorus seemed nearer in age, less intimidating, more of an equal, more... more approachable.

She touched her lips again. They still tingled.

Definitely more approachable.

It was only much later that she realized that her wonder at Apollodorus' attentions—and her reaction to them—had filled her mind so completely that it had momentarily obliterated the memory of her ordeal at Ptolemy XIV's hands.

She turned to her side and didn't even notice the ache in her shoulders and back. Bast resettled herself in the curl of her stomach and started to purr again.

Kinglet, she thought.

They slept.

6

on the morning of the First Day of the Third Week
at the Sixth Hour…

S he rose with the sun at First Hour and lay for a moment
rejoicing that she had lived to see Ra begin his journey
across the sky once again. She was stiff and sore when
she rose and Keren tutted over her bruises, anointing them
with some tincture that felt better than it smelled but did
begin immediately to ease her soreness.

"Lucky none of these blows broke the skin," Keren
said.

Lucky for her Apollodorus had come before they'd had
broken out the whips, Tetisheri thought. She wondered if
the slave boy who had dropped the tray had lived to see the
sunrise. Probably not, and her heart grieved for him because
surely none would in Ptolemy Theos' court.

She dressed and went to break her fast with Uncle Neb

and Keren. Her uncle frowned at her. "Where were you yesterday? I had to put off finishing the inventory."

"I'm sorry, Uncle," she said with real repentance, because taking inventory, while essential to a well-run business, was much less fun than buying and selling. "A friend had a problem and needed my help." If this investigation went on for much longer she was going to have to work up some believable excuses for where she'd been and what she'd been doing to satisfy Neb. All the more reason to conclude it swiftly.

Something in that careful statement must have hinted him away from the topic because he changed the subject. "Keren tells me we have a new house guest."

"Yes. Have you seen her yet?"

"He hasn't," Keren said, "because I can't convince her to sit at the same table with a man. So she is eating in the kitchen with Phoebe."

"Has she decided on a name?"

"She doesn't have a name?' Uncle Neb said.

"She refuses to be called by the name her former master gave her."

Something in Keren's expression as she looked at Tetisheri made Uncle Neb ask, "And who was her former master?"

Keren looked at Tetisheri, who sighed. "Hunefer. I, ah, expropriated her from him last night."

Nebenteru and Keren exchanged concerned glances. "You saw Hunefer last night?" he said.

"Not voluntarily," she said. "This cheese is excellent. I

wonder where Phoebe got it." She helped herself to more bread and oil.

Neb broke the silence before it became that much more awkward. "I have meetings all morning in the Emporium. Can I trust you to conclude the inventory?"

"Of course, Uncle." Tetisheri grinned. "I can't wait to wade through the loot you brought home from upriver."

"Wait till you see the herbs!" Keren said. "I don't know what half of them are. I'm going to take samples to the Library this morning to see if they are listed in any of the herbals."

After breakfast Tetisheri visited the kitchen, where their guest was rolling out pastry under Phoebe's direction. There were already two trays piled high with tiny savory pastries stuffed with anchovies and spinach and cheese, and a large basket full of green grapes with the dew still on them sat in the sink.

Their cook, Phoebe, a thin, energetic Greek woman originally from Athens, looked up. "Ah, Tetisheri," she said. "The dough likes our new friend."

A bit of the dough adhered affectionately to their new friend's nose and more down the front of what was obviously one of Phoebe's old tunics, belted with an old faded scarf wrapped three times around the girl's waist. "Good morning... you know, you're really going to need a name. Any ideas?"

The girl cast a sideways look at Phoebe, who said, "I've been telling her about our gods. She seems taken by the story of Nike. She likes that Nike fought. And has wings."

"And Phoebe has seen a statue of her," the girl said unexpectedly. Her Greek was pure Alexandrian. She had to have spent most of her life in the city learning it.

"At Samothraki?" Tetisheri said. "Yes, it is spectacular. Uncle Neb has a picture of her hanging somewhere in the house."

"I showed her," Phoebe said.

"I will go see the statue myself one day."

"Ah." Tetisheri looked the girl over critically. "So, Nike. You'll need some clothes of your own. We can go to a clothier I know this afternoon. Would you like that?"

Nike shrugged.

"I'll take her when we're done with the pie," Phoebe said, looking amused.

"All right. Do you know how to read, Nike?"

Another shrug.

"You will learn to read," Tetisheri said sternly. "Keren and I will tutor you until you feel comfortable enough to attend a class."

The girl's voice dropped so low that Tetisheri had to strain to hear her. "If I go outside he might find me and take me back."

"You don't belong to him anymore, Nike." Nike shrank against Phoebe's side, and Tetisheri tried to moderate her tone. "You are now a member of our house. You are safe anywhere in Alexandria."

Nike looked unconvinced, but they always did at first.

Before she could go into the vast warehouse and give the

inventory of new goods the concentration it deserved, she wrote a note to the family scribe, Sheftu, instructing him to send the market price of one ten-year-old slave to the House of Hunefer along with a brief contract of purchase. Hunefer would remember Sheftu from the divorce. She anticipated no problems.

She folded and sealed the letter and took it to find a courier, and found herself stopped at the main door to the house, unable to open it.

If I go outside he might find me and take me back.

Her jaw tightened. By now Apollodorus would have informed the queen of the previous evening's events. She in turn would have instructed her brother as to how her friends would be treated by him in future. Probably in some public way that would be as humiliating as it would be infuriating.

Kinglet.

She felt a smile forming on her face, and it was easy, after all, to open the door and step outside into the street. She walked the missive to the corner courier service and stood for a moment, watching the boy hurry down the Way with the note clutched in his hand. The sun was warm and she raised her face to it, eyes closed, letting the events of the night before fall away, replaced by the hurry and bustle of another day in the city.

Well. All the events save one. She opened her eyes again and returned home slowly, the memory of Apollodorus' lips and hands and body as startling as it was arousing. She paused before their door and touched her lips with the tip of one finger. They felt entirely unlike the lips that she'd lived with for the previous nineteen years. And her body, too, seemed somehow more vibrant in every part, more alive, more awake. Hopeful, even. There was a vague memory at the back of her mind of long ago, when she was young and immortal, when she had last felt like this. When she had entertained certain thoughts of the handsome young guard assigned to her friend and queen.

Before her marriage, and the stillbirth of her child.

Keren opened the door abruptly and Tetisheri nearly fell inside.

"Sheri! I'm sorry, I didn't know—"

Tetisheri had not had time enough to rearrange her expression into something approaching serenity and Keren said sharply, "What's wrong? Sheri?"

Tetisheri took a breath and summoned up a smile. "It's nothing. Really." She noticed the basket in Keren's hand. "You're off to the Library with your herbs, then? I'll be interested to hear what you find out." She stepped inside and shut the door firmly between them.

Neb's foreman was rearranging the antiquities section of the warehouse—there was a particularly fine bust of Artemis she hadn't seen before whose style looked to predate Scopas, if not Praxiteles. The latest shipment was stacked in the staging area against the dock wall. There were small jars with airtight wax seals full to the brim with pepper and cloves and nutmeg and cinnamon from Maluku, the aforementioned baskets of dried herbs from Punt, copper cookware from Bactria, large spindles of silk thread from Sinae ready to be dyed and woven here in Alexandria. There was a bundle of ebony planks, planed but not finished, and a dozen elephant tusks which must have cost Uncle Neb the equivalent of the price of the *Hapi* but for which they would earn back ten times the cost when they turned them over. There was a small, heavy chest full of lapis lazuli, also from Bactria, and another of, unbelievably, white jade, the purest and most highly valued color of that gemstone, one that almost never made it out of Sinae and certainly not in a commercial quantity such as this.

Riches, indeed, and Tetisheri spent the morning happily cataloguing the contents and directing the staff to store them in the appropriate places, a job which felt far more comfortable than the one the queen had assigned her the day before. The spices, jade, and tusks were locked safely away under her direct supervision in the strong room built into the shared wall between warehouse and home. She carried her lists to the office to enter them into the account books to estimate the import tax due the throne. Friendship was one thing but business was something else entirely, and Cleopatra was still paying off the massive sums her father had borrowed from the Romans to take back his throne. The queen was known to extract the smallest coin owed her by whatever means necessary, up to and including confiscation of such property as satisfied the sum set by the royal tax commissioner, imprisonment of the offender, and, in especially egregious cases, torture and even death, which

sentence was enacted in public as a warning to others foolish enough to attempt to cheat their sovereign out of her
just due. Even if the task the queen had set before Tetisheri
had been requested as a favor instead of a royal command,
Cleopatra had made no promise of material reward and
Tetisheri had no realistic expectation of same. She checked
her figures twice.

Bast was sitting motionless on the minute square of desk
top where the sun shone the strongest, watching the movement of Tetisheri's stylus as it scratched across the papyrus.
A claw flicked out and the stylus sailed into a corner.

"You," Tetisheri told her, "are a nuisance. I shall lodge a
complaint with your mother." She touched the pendant at
her throat.

Bast yawned, unalarmed.

"Was that a comment on my figures? My penmanship?
Approval of my determination to pay the queen her due?"

Bast tidied her whiskers and resumed her impression of a
statue. Tetisheri fetched the stylus and sat back down again.

Her morning tasks were routine enough that they occupied only the front of her mind. In the meantime, the back
of her mind worked at the queen's task.

The theft had been perfectly orchestrated. The thieves
had known when the coins would arrive, on what ship, and
where that ship would dock.

She raised her head and stared out the window that looked
onto a little walled garden where Phoebe raised flowers and
herbs. The roses were nearly spent but a few blooms lingered,

scenting the light breeze that crept in through the window unannounced.

The thieves would have been better informed even than that, she thought. Good plans took time, and this had been a very good plan. They had to have known that the coins were to be struck in the first place, and where. They would have to have known when they would have been ready to be shipped and when they would arrive in Alexandria. They had to have arranged a secure hiding place because the coins had vanished into the city without a trace, and what's more, without the whisper of a rumor of their theft. Such a rumor would ordinarily have spread around the city like wildfire and inspired every aspiring treasure hunter within the city walls to try their hand at finding it and stealing it for themselves.

Such a robbery was not something invented on the instant, an opportunistic snatch-and-grab. Apollodorus and by extension the queen vouched for Laogonus' integrity and there were enough suspects already that Tetisheri was willing to trust in that judgement, at least for the present. She still wanted to talk to his crew, though. The queen's agent on Cyprus she knew nothing of and ships traveled between there and Alexandria daily. It would have been easy enough for him to pass on information from Lemesos and even to coordinate the theft. Apollodorus was right—he must either be summoned back to Alexandria or Tetisheri would have to go to Lemesos.

And then there was Khemit. While the existence of the Eye of Isis was the stuff of legend in Alexandria and Egypt, the

Eye's identity was never generally known, for his or her own protection, and for the access anonymity lent to any investigation. But whoever killed her had to have known who she was and what she did for the queen, and that Cleopatra had given her the job of finding the thieves and retrieving the new issue.

Tetisheri was certain that she had, and that they had killed her for it.

The inescapable conclusion was that someone in the queen's confidence had betrayed her trust.

Why?

So far, Tetisheri could identify only two motives. One, common greed, was simple and easy to understand. There were always those who wanted more than they had, and who preferred stealing to earning. A shipment of new currency would be an irresistible target. But greed alone as a motive for crossing Cleopatra VII's will? For stealing from a queen who was proving to be the most fiscally prudent Ptolemy in their entire three-hundred-year dynasty? A queen who had already demonstrated by her treatment of tax cheats what she thought of robbing the royal treasury? It was difficult to conceive of such foolishness. Although Maat above knew that one of the first things a beginning trader learned was that the world was full of cheats who believed implicitly that they would never be caught and who were always astonished when they were.

The other motive would be political and more difficult to substantiate, but one Tetisheri found far more likely given the current climate. The theft could have been intended to undercut the Alexandrian economy, just now beginning to regain its footing after the improvidences of Ptolemy Auletes and the subsequent wars of succession. As the winner of those wars, Cleopatra had more enemies than friends and some of the most dangerous of them were close kin.

The Ptolemies bred for blood, not brains.

"Mmrow?"

Tetisheri realized she had said the words out loud. "My apologies for disturbing your meditation," she said gravely.

Bast sniffed, possibly in agreement with Apollodorus' sentiments, and resumed her resemblance to a graven image.

If anything, last night's audience with Ptolemy XIV had only underscored Apollodorus' dictum. She shifted on her stool. The ache in her back and shoulders was easing courtesy of Keren's salve. She wondered fleetingly if Keren might like to make and package it in retail quantities.

She reined in her wandering attention. No, it would take much less time to make a list of the queen's friends than it would a list of her enemies. Nevertheless, Tetisheri pulled out a fresh sheet of papyrus and began to do just that, beginning with the queen's siblings, Ptolemy XIV and her sister Arsinoë IV, now held captive in Rome against the day of Julius Caesar's triumph, when she would be paraded in his train and then strangled. She added a number of Alexandrian nobles for any number of reasons, including Hunefer and his mother (it wasn't just because she wanted them to be guilty, she told herself) and pretty much every Roman citizen with the slightest pretense to power on either side of the Middle Sea. Too many of them would benefit from a destabilization of Cleopatra's rule and the subsequent diminution of Caesar's power. Even better, removing her from her throne all together—after all, she had lost it once already, and if their history lessons had taught them anything, citizens not having enough money to buy food for their families was a powerful tool with which to break a reign.

A knock sounded. She put the list aside gladly. "Yes?" The door opened and she looked up to behold Nike in the doorway. A Nike transformed by a bath, a brand new knee-length linen tunic dyed a luscious red that set off her dark skin to admiration, a narrow, braided leather belt buckled neatly round her waist, and braided leather sandals on her feet. She had cut her hair, too, so that it formed a smaller, neater cloud around her face instead of that tumble halfway down her back. Tetisheri rather missed the tumble.

She preened beneath Tetisheri's admiring gaze.

"Yes?" Tetisheri said blandly.

"You have a visitor," Nike said. She stood very straight, chin up, shoulders back, hands clasped formally before her. All that was missing was the crown, but that would have been superfluous—one would never dare trifle with a person of such immense dignity. "He gives his name as Aurelius Cotta, and begs you to favor him with a few moments of your time. He waits for you in the atrium."

Cotta. Caesar's most trusted aide. The man with the scar she had stumbled over on their way out of Cleopatra's presence the previous morning. This could not be good. "Thank you," Tetisheri said. "Please tell him I will be with him directly."

Nike bent her head and whisked off. Tetisheri grinned at her receding back and turned to tidy her desk and lock away her notes. It would never do to allow these Romans to think they could summon an Egyptian citizen with the snap of their fingers, especially in that citizen's own home. She neatened her desk, waited for Bast to decide if she would accompany Tetisheri to greet this Roman, and took her time walking to the atrium so as not to be construed to be in any way out of breath.

He stood very much where Apollodorus had stood the previous morning, by the fountain, watching the water trickle from one level of marble tier to the next. It was near the Sixth Hour and from directly overhead the light of the sun poured through the compluvium and erased any lingering shadows. He raised his head when he heard her step, and contemplated her for a few moments. She refused to fidget beneath that encompassing stare. Bast leapt up on the bench in front of the fountain, unerringly found the spot where the sun was strongest, and began to wash.

"So," he said. "Caesar was right. Not a cook."

He spoke in Latin and she responded in kind. "I'm sorry, sir. I don't believe we've been introduced."

"Instead, a merchant," he said, "and a partner in a flourishing concern. Extraordinary. Women aren't merchants in Rome."

"No," she said. "They are wives and mothers. And,

sometimes, if they are very, very good, they might be allowed to weave a length of linen."

He did not leap to the defense of Rome's superior social mores as she half expected he might. "You've been to Rome, then, lady," he said, his affability unruffled. "If nothing else your Latin gives you away. You sound like Cicero at his most poisonous. My compliments. Perhaps you accompanied the queen when she was there with her father some years ago?"

"I'm a merchant, sir. A facility for languages is necessary in my business." She raised her chin. "If you won't introduce yourself, may I ask why you are here?"

"Come, come," he said, "you know very well who I am." He pointed at his scar. "Everyone knows who I am." The blow had shattered Cotta's helmet and left him with a white scar that twisted up his left eyebrow and the outer corner of his left eye and pulled his entire face a little off-center, giving him a look of perpetual skepticism.

That look was now bent on her. If it was meant to intimidate it failed. She did not escort him to the more comfortably appointed receiving room reserved for honored guests. She did not offer him refreshments. She didn't even ask him to sit down on one of the benches ringing the fountain. She simply stood, squarely in front of the door that led deeper into the house and not coincidentally blocking it, hands clasped demurely before her, a look of carefully cultivated polite inquiry on her face. If anything, she was very probably giving a good imitation of Nike's new-found gravitas. "Again, sir," she said, controlling a quivering lip, "how may I help you?"

He cocked an eyebrow. "What have I said, I wonder, that amuses you so?"

Damn the man. Romans as a race were usually very jealous of their dignity, ready to take offense at even the mildest joke ventured at their expense. Any other Roman would have stamped out in a huff by now, but this one persisted in having a sense of humor. "Very well, Aurelius Cotta," she said. "Yes, I know who you are, and—"

"And just to save time, we met briefly yesterday in the private apartments of Queen Cleopatra. My general wishes to know why the queen felt it necessary not to introduce him to such an old and dear friend." He correctly identified the look in her eye and said soothingly, "Yes, yes, you'd like to say that Caesar has no claim on the obedience of a loyal subject of the queen of Alexandria and Egypt." His smile, too, was twisted up by the scar. "But we both know that for the fiction it is, do we not?"

"I find it odd that it took you this long to threaten me."

"You noticed! Excellent." He waited.

She smiled at him. It was not the effort it should have been. "I will not put my words into the queen's mouth, Aurelius Cotta, for my head enjoys its present location. I have no idea why she didn't introduce me to Caesar. She sent for me—"

"By way of her very own personal guard, Apollodorus. An interesting man, that. Another partner in another flourishing concern. Yet another Alexandrian success story, although he is not native to the city."

He paused invitingly. She said nothing. "There is little

known of him or his companions before they arrived in Alexandria, what, over ten years ago? And so soon in the king's confidence, so much so that he was named his heir's personal guard."

A frisson of unease ran up her spine. This man was far too observant and far too close to Caesar. Any interest he showed in anyone, including herself and anyone close to her, would best be deflected, however that might be accomplished. "The queen sent for me as she sometimes does—"

"He is known as Apollodorus the Sicilian, but all the Sicilians I know are small and dark, whereas he is tall and fair," he said meditatively. "I would imagine those green eyes have slain more than their fair share of hearts over the years."

Tetisheri felt the heat climb up the back of her neck beneath his interested gaze and felt her temper rise with it. "The queen sent for me," she said for the third time, with an outward calm that took a concerted effort to maintain, "as she sometimes does when she has a free moment, and we revisited old times over a light lunch." She shrugged. "There really is nothing more sinister in our meeting than that. Now if you will excuse me—"

Instead, he took a turn around the fountain, hands clasped behind his back. He came to a stop in front of her again. "Would it have had something to do with you being haled before King Ptolemy last night?"

A brief silence. "You, sir," she said, "are irritatingly well informed."

"It is my invariable habit," he said, and looked as surprised as she felt when she laughed. It alleviated at least some of the tension that had been building in the room. "Having revealed so much, perhaps I should reveal all," he said, and sat down on the broad seat in front of the fountain without invitation. He patted the marble next to him, one eyebrow raised. Prudently, she remained where she was. He sighed. "Very well, then. We know that the queen ordered a new issue of drachma from Cyprus. We know also that that shipment was stolen right out of the ship it was carried in the morning after it arrived in the Great Harbor." He looked for her response. She gave none. He tsked impatiently. "We also know that the queen has set inquiries in motion to find the thieves and recover the coins, and that one of her agents was murdered here in Alexandria not two mornings ago."

He rose to his feet and strolled forward. "And practically before the corpse was cold, the queen sent for you. I believe she has asked you to take up the dead agent's task. Am I correct?"

Saying nothing seemed the safest avenue.

He put his finger under her chin and raised it so he could look straight into her eyes. "There is no threat here, lady, to either you, your mistress, or her coin. Caesar has a vested interest in a stable Egyptian economy, which will be much better suited to delivering the grain to Rome on time. I offer you assistance only."

"You will remove your hand from my person, sir," she said. "At once."

There was something in her face that wiped the smile from

his. He stepped back, palms out. "My apologies, lady. I meant no offense."

"You gave it nonetheless," she said. "Goodbye, sir."

"Good day," he said, "but not, I think, goodbye." He bowed slightly, but before he turned to leave he cast a glance over her from head to toe, lingering here and there and coming to rest on her face for a long moment.

If Apollodorus had not kissed her the night before, if she had not responded to him in the way that she had, she would not have recognized the look in Cotta's eyes now.

It was appreciation, not as a sparring partner, an enemy of Rome or even as a possible source of information, but as a woman.

And it was desire.

7

*on the morning of the First Day of the Third Week
at the Seventh Hour...*

"Well, and what was all that about?"

Tetisheri was recalled to the present by her uncle's voice. She took a moment to assume a calm expression before she turned. "Nothing of importance, Uncle," she said indifferently. "Someone I met yesterday renewing the acquaintance."

The pearl at the tip of his beard waggled in disbelief. "Nothing to do with the business, then?"

"No." The tone of her voice stopped that line of inquiry stone dead. Neb was wise in the ways of his niece and the pearl stilled. "I finished the inventory and updated our accounts. Would you mind if I stepped out for a bit? I shouldn't be gone too long."

He waved a hand. "So long as you're back in time for the reception and auction this evening."

It took her a moment to remember. Uncle Neb always hosted a reception for his best customers a day or two after he returned from a buying trip, the centerpiece of the evening a brief auction of half a dozen or more of the best pieces he had acquired. Which explained the mass production of pastries in the kitchen this morning.

"You forgot!" he said, and threw up his hands.

"Of course I didn't forget, Uncle," she said untruthfully. "I'll be back in plenty of time."

"You need to be here, Tetisheri." He sighed, the pearl signaling his impatience with her lack of enthusiasm. "I don't understand why you hate these things so much. Everyone loves you and looks forward to seeing you."

"How nice," she said with no sincerity whatever. "I'll be back in time, I promise."

He grumbled something and she scuttled out of the room and the house before he decided she needed to help Phoebe with the preparations. She was only slightly less inept at cooking than she was at socializing.

Ra was past his zenith and Alexandria had returned to work. Children splashed in the fountains and played kickball in the parks. Mothers gossiped together as they watched. Slaves rushed about on errands, coarsely woven bags over their shoulders and baskets on their backs and heads. Men haggled with vendors over the price of any and everything for sale, and scholars argued philosophy on every corner surrounded by a gaggle of students hanging on their every word.

It was a peaceful scene, a day like any other, and yet,

as she had the day before, Tetisheri sensed an underlying tension, as if the city were on edge, waiting. For what? To all outward appearances their queen had effectively tamed Caesar, bound him to her with an heir, and contrived to put his legions at her service. In spite of their Roman, ah, guardian's determination to prove the fiction that was their co-rulership, it was known down to the grubbiest slave turning a spit at the humblest kitchen fire that Ptolemy XIV was a king in name only and that the true power resided with his sister. A sister with a more comprehensive understanding of the city and country she ruled that her ancestors had even attempted to share, and one totally ignored by her brother. There wasn't a single Ptolemy in three centuries whose subjects hadn't risen up in rebellion against their ruler, along the Nile and even in the very streets of Alexandria itself. But not this Ptolemy. Not yet, anyway.

Alexandria, in fact, was in a more stable situation than it had been in generations, and in a more autonomous one, too.

But still, the city held its breath. Tetisheri wondered what it knew that she didn't.

Aristander was in his office and agreed to show her the place where Khemit had been murdered and from there to take her to where Laogonus' crew was being kept.

"Gives me an excuse to get some air," he said when she thanked him. Outside, on the Way, he stood for a moment to draw in a deep breath of that air. He wet his finger and held it up. "A nice, steady, onshore breeze. Be a beautiful day for a sail."

"It would at that." When he raised an eyebrow at her wistful tone, she smiled. "One of Uncle Neb's receptions this evening. My attendance is mandatory."

He laughed. "Ah yes, I remember how well you like social events. Cleopatra used to have to command your presence at them so she didn't have to suffer empty compliments from bootlickers hopeful for favor or advancement all by herself."

"Yes, well, Uncle Neb seems to have taken her example to heart," she said, and he chuckled and began to walk.

She fell into step next to him. "Any word of the lost shipment?" she said in a low voice.

"None. That's what is so frustrating. A theft of this magnitude and political importance is impossible to hide, or so I would have thought. As you know, my dear Tetisheri, I don't believe in conspiracies, or at least not in conspiracies that can be kept secret. People always have to talk—to their friends, their wives, their mistresses. The impulse to boast is irresistible. But my men have been squeezing their informants from Rhakotis to the Jewish Quarter for seven solid days. They have not raised so much as a whisper." He shook his head. "Unprecedented, believe me."

"It's fatal information for anyone to have."

"That might be why," he said, and their eyes met in perfect understanding. No one wanted to be in the middle when the hidden conflict between Cleopatra and Ptolemy erupted into the open, and if Ptolemy were in any way involved in the theft of the coin there was a very good chance it might.

In which case the blood would run in the city streets. No one wanted it to be their blood. "There," he said, halting. "Her body was found by the street sweeper just there."

He indicated a corner where a narrow side street met the Street of the Soma, a shorter, less grand version of the Way that ran north–south down the center of the city.

"How was her body left?"

"She was hit from behind. She fell forward, her arms outstretched."

"As if to catch herself."

"Yes. Her hands were a little chafed, and her elbows."

"So she was alive when she fell, which means this is where she was struck down."

His eyebrows went up. "But how else could it have happened?"

"She could have been struck down somewhere else and her body brought here. Was there any blood?"

"Yes. Head wounds always bleed copiously."

"Which confirms the theory that she was struck down here. The single blow to her head was her only wound?"

"As you saw."

"But could she have been struck a second time, after she fell?" Before he could answer she hurried on. "I ask only because if she was struck once and left to lie here, as Apollodorus pointed out, her attacker could have meant something other than murder. If she was struck again, as she lay, he could only have meant murder."

"Zotikos said nothing of a second blow."

She bit her lip. "Would you mind if I sent someone else to examine the wound?"

He thought, one finger tapping his lips. "All right. But if Zotikos hears of it—"

"Not from me, he won't," she said, relieved. She had been afraid that Aristander would be offended by what could be presumed to be a slight on the professionalism of his department.

"Or from me." He grinned at her.

The four crewmen were being held in a nondescript house on the periphery of the Royal Palace complex. Armed guards stood at every door and window. "Sergeant," Aristander said to the one on the front door.

"Sir." The guard snapped to attention.

"Any trouble?"

"We're ready for it if it comes, sir."

Tetisheri got the impression the sergeant was rather hoping for said trouble to manifest itself, and soon. It had to be very boring, to be constantly on guard against a threat that never came.

"Carry on. Tetisheri?"

He held the door for her.

There were two more guards inside, along with the four crewmen, sitting in a circle dicing for what looked like a very small collection of very small coins, none of them silver or gold. The two guards saw Aristander and shot to their feet. He waved off their apologies. "Gentlemen, here is Tetisheri, come to question you as regards recent events." He nodded at a door that led into a back room. "You know the drill. One at a time, Debu first."

"Lucky Debu," one of them said, grinning, and was kicked by a crewmate. "What? All I said was that he was lucky." He winked at her.

Tetisheri could feel his eyes on her backside all the way through the door.

The room contained a small table and two stools, and had no window. There was nothing in it to distract anyone's attention from the questions and answers being given inside these four walls. Tetisheri wondered if Aristander had had this house built for this specific purpose. "Please," she said, indicating the table. She sat down opposite Debu and folded her hands in her lap, regarding him openly across the table. He folded his arms and looked back. He was Egyptian, short and bulky but with muscle, not fat. His skin was a weather-beaten bronze and his eyes deep set and crinkled at the corners from years of keeping watch for squalls, or pirates, or Romans, or any number of the other hazards to navigation that plagued the Middle Sea.

His knuckles were cut and swollen and there was a large bruise turning yellow on his jaw. He met her eyes calmly, without apprehension, and waited for her to speak first.

"The queen has asked me to make inquiries as to the theft the *Thalassa* suffered last week."

"We have all already spoken to the Eye."

"Yes," she said, "you have, and now you will speak to me."

A flash of something that might have been humor crossed his face. "I serve at the queen's command."

"Your queen appreciates your service," she said, inclining her head, although she doubted very much if Cleopatra had ever had Debu's name spoken out loud in her presence. From the look in his eyes he was thinking the same thing.

But with equal gravity he said, "How may I best serve the queen in this instance?"

"The *Thalassa* is a courier on the queen's business."

He inclined his head. "That is our mission, yes."

"Have you made other trips like this one to Lemesos?"

"We have."

"And your orders come always through Laogonus."

"They do."

"And you meet the same person at Lemesos docks each time?"

"We do." He shifted. "That is, the queen's agent is always the same person. The carriers differ on occasion."

"How often?"

He shrugged. "Once the agent switched to camels some-one had imported from Antioch. The road down to Lemesos is very steep and little wider than a goat track. Usually the shipments are conveyed by donkey, and sometimes they lose one over the side, with no hope of recovery as the weight of these shipments take chests and donkeys straight to the bottom. The agent said he was hoping there would be less wastage with camels."

Tetisheri, always interested in anything to do with the shipment of goods and the means thereof, said, "And was there?"

"No." He grinned. "Everyone on the island hated the camels. They bite and spit and evidently when they're really annoyed they urinate on the person standing nearest them."

Tetisheri couldn't help but grin back. "The agent?"

"I believe that may have been the case," he said. "He certainly used some very inventive language to describe the experience."

Tetisheri took a moment to compose herself. "Please tell me everything that happened to do with this particular shipment, beginning with when you first heard of it."

"On the Ninth Day of First Week, Laogonus called the crew together to tell us we would be sailing for Lemesos the next day at First Hour. We had fair winds and made landfall on..."

And Debu proceeded to tell a story that in matched Laogonus' in nearly every particular. So did the story told by the other three crewmen, Old Pert the Pict, Leon the Iberian (and the flirt), and Bolgios the Gaul, large and taciturn with enormous hands made to haul on lines. All of them sported cuts and bruises of the same age and stage of healing as the first mate's. They had not given up their cargo without a fight, "but," Debu had said, "there were so many of them. They swarmed up over the side and we were so busy fighting the fire they were in the hold almost before we knew it."

She sat for a moment after Bolgios had left the room, frowning at the opposite wall. The crew were as one deeply angry about the theft but appeared unafraid of being accused of it or blamed for it. Debu had been born in Alexandria. Pert and Leon and Bolgios had immigrated there as children. There was nothing to choose among their stories and, lacking evidence to the contrary, they were to a man exactly and precisely what they seemed to be—an experienced, responsible, loyal crew who took whatever the queen wanted taken swiftly and efficiently to wherever she wanted it to go. And they were discreet, too, a quality the queen would value above all else. They had volunteered no information unless Tetisheri specifically asked for it, including any hints as to the kinds of cargoes they might have carried at other times to other destinations.

The door opened and she looked up. Aristander came in and sat across from her. "Well?"

"I can find no discrepancies in any of their stories. What do you know of their personal lives?"

"All are married but Pert, who is a widower. All have children apprenticed to various trades. Pert's eldest daughter owns her own taverna."

"Edeva's?"

"You know it?"

"I was there last night," she said. "What else?"

He shrugged. "All but Pert own comfortable homes not far from the waterfront. Pert sold his to finance his daughter's business. None of them have any outstanding debts."

"How much are they paid?" Aristander told her, and she raised her eyebrows. "And I thought we were generous."

"The queen's feeling is that if she pays them well enough they won't steal from her. I must say I have some sympathy for that viewpoint." He looked at her and said again, "Well?"

She shook her head. "They all have far too much to lose to be involved in this. But someone who knew about the shipment was. It is the only possible explanation. This was a theft that was planned from the very moment the queen gave the order for the coin to be struck." She held up her hand, ticking off her fingers. "Who knew? The queen, Sosigenes, the queen's agent on Cyprus, the craftsmen who actually made the coin. Probably the carriers had some notion. Laogonus and his crew. Who else?"

He spread his hands.

She nodded. "I think I should talk to the agent."

"On Cyprus? Shall he be brought here, or—"

"I'd rather go to Cyprus and interview him there. That way he won't have time to make up a story." Aristander smiled. "What?"

"You think like a shurta."

She laughed. "The highest of compliments!"

"Indeed. Shall you take your own ship?"

"No," she said, thinking it over. "No, I believe the *Thalassa* will do."

"Isn't it undergoing repairs? They suffered some damage from the fire."

"Laogonus said they were almost finished, and I would

like to be present as the crew makes the same passage they did prior to the theft. They might remember something they have forgotten."

He nodded. "And Apollodorus will accompany you."

"Oh, but—"

He shook his head. "No, Sheri. Apollodorus will accompany you. I'm sure the queen would agree."

She was sure the queen would, too. "Very well," she said with a sigh.

"I'll send him word."

She rose and marched out of the house, if not precisely in a huff then in something perilously close to it.

It wasn't that she didn't want to see Apollodorus again, because of course she did. She shivered, thinking of the touch of his warm, hard hands on her body, of his assurance in the way he had held her. He was obviously more experienced in the pleasures of the flesh than she was, who had until now only associated the act with fear and pain.

She could not have said in that moment whether she wanted or feared their next meeting. It infuriated her that she was nervous about it, though.

She walked in the door at the Eleventh Hour precisely to be swept up in the preparations for the reception, which resembled a haboob minus the sand. Nike, looking regal, laden with a teetering stack of little plates, almost collided with Keren, looking put upon, carrying a tray filled with bowls of halloumi, tashi, muttabal, and hummus. Phoebe, looking harassed, followed with two large decorative baskets filled with the savory pastries Tetisheri had seen in the kitchen that morning. She snatched one and then had to juggle it from hand to hand as it was fresh from the oven.

"Tetisheri!" Nebenteru said, looking indignant. "You aren't even dressed!"

"I know, Uncle, I'm sorry, I'll be quick."

"See that you are!" He swept from the room, the pearl jutting out in condemnation.

"Keren? When you're done, please come to my room? I need to ask a favor."

Keren, intent on not scattering mezes from the atrium to the docks, nodded, and Tetisheri escaped to her room. Bast was a black curl on her pillow and looked up in annoyance at Tetisheri's precipitous entry. "Yes, yes, forgive me for interrupting your pre-sleep nap, but some of us have stupid parties to ready ourselves for."

She shed her clothes, tucked the Eye beneath her pillow— Bast cast her a baleful look—and cleaned herself quickly with a cloth and a basin of lukewarm water that one of the wonderful women of the house must have left for her. A silk dress had been laid out for her, a work of art woven in gold and green with straps over the shoulders and a straight neckline. It was cut very close to her figure and she eyed the result with apprehension.

"Oh, Sheri, it's lovely on you! I knew it would be!" Keren came in and shut the door behind her.

"A little too lovely, if you ask me." The nipples of her breasts were perfectly outlined by the silk. "I can't wear this, Keren."

"Nonsense! You have a lovely figure which most of the time can't even be seen in those baggy tunics you wear. Where's your jewelry?" She rifled impatiently in the little wooden chest on the table. "The very thing!" She held up a wide collar strung with a thousand tiny beads of citrine and amethyst, with a large gold clasp in the shape of a cat. "Take off your necklace."

"I always wear my necklace."

"Not tonight, you don't. Off."

Tetisheri put her hands on her hips and glared. "I thought you were a doctor, not a lady's maid."

"And I thought you were nearly twenty, not ten. Take it off so I can put this on."

Bast, engaged in a thorough washing of her left hind leg, looked up and meowed in unmistakable agreement. Tetisheri transferred her glare. "Traitor!" Fuming, she fumbled at the back of her pendant and handed it over. Keren replaced it with the collar. "Excellent," she said with satisfaction. "Now your bracelets." In spite of Tetisheri's inarticulate protest four narrow, highly polished gold bracelets were shoved inexorably over her hands, two above her elbows and two around her wrists. "Now the fillet. Oh gods, your hair!"

Tetisheri, peering into the silvered mirror on the wall, had to admit that it was rather a mess, and submitted to having a wide-toothed ivory comb dragged ruthlessly through it. When Keren was done Tetisheri's eyes were watering but her hair was a shining black curtain that just touched her shoulders.

Standing behind her, Keren settled the thin gold fillet over her forehead. "Look." Keren turned her to face the mirror again. "There," she said with satisfaction. "You look a proper lady of the house."

A stranger, pretty, a lady even, stared back at her with startled eyes. The last time she'd worn silk it had been forced on her by Ipwet for a formal dinner in Hunefer's house. She had been heavily pregnant at the time, her face puffy, her hands and feet swollen, incapable of being more than one room away from the chamber pot. The dress had been a garish weave so loud it could have been seen outside at the dark of the moon, and there had never been any hope of it fitting.

This was an altogether different woman.

"Not bad, eh?" Keren said, smiling.

"No."

Keren laughed. "Don't sound so surprised." She herself wore a gown fashioned in the style of her homeland made of raw silk dyed the red of pomegranates, with a stola in a gold and blue weave draped over her shoulder and belted to her waist. Her mass of black curls was held back with a wide band of ivory openwork and she wore large gold hoops in her ears. "I'm sorry, in all the excitement I forgot to ask. How are you feeling?"

"All right." She met Keren's skeptical eyes and shrugged. "A little sore still. Does anything show?" She craned her head to squint at her back.

"No. The straps are wide enough and the bodice is high enough to hide all your bruises." Keren hugged her, with care, her eyes sparkling. "Neb did well by the womenfolk of the household on that last trip to Antioch, didn't he? And did you see Nike?"

"You mean Her Majesty?"

Keren laughed. "Well, let's go show ourselves off!" She caught Tetisheri's hand and headed for the door, only to be pulled to an abrupt stop. "Sheri, we have to go. People are already arriving and you know how Neb gets when we're late for anything."

"Just give me one moment," Tetisheri said, closing the door again. "I need a favor."

Keren opened her mouth to argue, saw Tetisheri's expression, and closed it again. "Of course, Tetisheri," she said soberly. "Whatever I can do."

"I need you to look at a corpse."

Keren blinked. "A corpse? As in someone already—dead?"

"Yes."

"Well," Keren said doubtfully. "As you know, my specialty is the living."

"Just look at her, please? I want to know how she died."

"'Her?'"

"Yes. A woman, a servant of the queen who died two days ago. I don't want to say anything more, I want your own observations uncolored by anything I might say." Keren didn't say anything and Tetisheri put a hand on her arm. "Please, Keren? I wouldn't ask if it weren't important."

Keren's face relaxed into a smile. "No, you wouldn't, and of course I will, Tetisheri. Where is this body?"

"The Shurta. Ask for Aristander. And don't let him tell you anything about her, either."

"Ah. A mystery. How delicious." Keren held up her hands to forestall Tetisheri's comment. "All right, all right, I'll go, first thing tomorrow morning." She opened the door. "Although in return, if you see that oily old satyr, Nymphodorus, slithering in my direction at any point during the evening, I expect a prompt rescue."

"Done."

8

*on the First Day of the Third Week
a little after the Twelfth Hour...*

As was Neb's custom, the central area of the warehouse had been cleared out. Every standing oil lamp between here and the Nile had been found, filled and lit, and the handsome set of carved mahogany doors that fronted Hermes Street had been unbarred and thrown wide. Tetisheri followed Keren through the adjoining door and locked it behind her, as always glad that Nebenteru's hospitality did not extend to guests having access to their home.

She turned, bumped into a hard chest, and looked up to see Apollodorus. "Oh," she said.

He himself had dressed for the occasion in a raw silk tunic dyed a rich brown, held at the waist by a finely tooled leather belt with a bronze buckle in the shape of the eye of Horus.

She dragged her eyes back up and found him grinning at her, and she felt a returning smile spread across her face unbidden. Nothing to be afraid of here, she thought, and felt another shiver ripple up her spine.

Dub saluted her from the door, Castus from one corner, Crixus another, and Is presided overall from the center of the room, his wild white curls tamed with pomade and possibly deliberately made to hint at horns standing up from the crown of his head. Faunus to the life, only rather more benign. None of them were armed but then they were as well known to Alexandrians as the queen herself. Belatedly Tetisheri remembered that Neb always hired the Five Soldiers as a preventative measure against theft, petty and otherwise, at these events.

Apollodorus ran a finger lightly over her neckline. "You look beautiful."

His finger left a line of fire on her skin and her heart was beating so hard so high up in her throat it was difficult to say words. She took a deep and she hoped calming breath. "Thank you," she said, and was pitifully proud she'd been able to get that much out without stuttering.

"How are you feeling?"

"Sore. Angry." She saw Keren giving them an odd look and felt her flush deepening. "I'm sorry I was late," she said more naturally, trying for an urbanity to match his own and certain she was failing miserably. "Is Uncle Neb fuming?"

"See for yourself." He nodded, and Tetisheri followed his

gaze to behold Uncle Neb, resplendent in a tunic woven of blue and silver threads and a large, tear-shaped pearl matching the one trembling on the tip of his beard hanging from his left earlobe. He looked every inch the successful merchant trader, supremely confident, condescendingly gracious, and overwhelmingly hospitable.

She smothered a laugh.

"That's better," Apollodorus said approvingly. "For a moment there I thought you were going to faint." Before she could deny it, she hoped with sincere indignation, he said, "Did your activities this afternoon bear fruit?"

"Only insofar as I am now sure we have to go to Lemesos to interview the queen's agent. And you? Did you find Atet?"

He shook his head. "No. I—"

Neb swooped down on them. "And here she is!" He gathered her to him in a one-armed hug. "Gentlemen and ladies, you all know my niece and full partner in Nebenteru's Luxury Goods." A chorus of greetings rose up from every group in the room. Tetisheri smiled and inclined her head in acknowledgement.

Neb, pearl stiff with pride, marched her over to an older gentleman who had gratified his host's vanity by dressing in his finest. "Tetisheri, you know Lord Amenemhet, Nomarch of the Crocodile, of course."

Tetisheri bowed low. "You honor us with your presence, lord."

"Nonsense!" Amenemhet, a big, bluff man with a red face

and a bombastic manner, caught up her hand and touched it to his forehead. "The honor is mine, lovely Tetisheri. It has been too long since you rolled out your treasures for all of Alexandria to admire." He kissed the back of her hand and waggled his eyebrows. "Yourself chief among them."

She laughed and so did he. She'd always liked Amenemhet. She exchanged greetings with Kiya, his smiling and indulgent wife, and promised to pay a call one afternoon soon.

A touch on her elbow brought her attention back to Uncle Neb. "And we have new friends as well. Tetisheri, allow me to make you known to a visitor from Rome, Gaius Cassius Longinus, and his sons, Naevius and Petronius. Gentlemen, my niece and partner, Tetisheri of House Nebenteru."

All three men had their heads inclined over full plates of Phoebe's delicious pastries when she turned. When they raised them, Tetisheri saw that they were the three Romans present at Ptolemy's court the night before.

It took them a few moments longer to recognize her in all her finery. When they did they froze momentarily in place.

"Ah," she said, giving them her very sweetest smile, "visitors from Rome. How wonderful that you chose to spend your evening with us, Cassian Longinus."

"Cassius," Uncle Neb murmured.

"Cloelius, of course, my apologies, sir." She turned her glittering smile on the two sons, who looked as if they didn't know whether to smile falsely or sneer. The sneer would seem to come more naturally. "And your two so promising sons. Please be welcome, gentlemen, and may I draw your attention to some very fine statues of household gods your host recently brought back from a trip upriver?"

She walked to the display and they followed her as if they'd been hypnotized. "You see? Small, exquisitely crafted, easily packed. The statue of Sobek the Crocodile I'm sure you will agree is particularly fine. Notice the citrine and nacre inlay. Sobek, of course, is also known as Lord of Faiyum, and is worshipped as the guardian of Egypt and is the patron god of our army."

One of the sons snorted audibly at this mention of Egypt's army, which admittedly had not covered itself with glory since the days of the Pharaohs.

She broadened her smile and added in a helpful voice, "Much like your Mars. Or Ares, as is I believe his original name." She added, apologetically, "From the Greek, you know. Most if not all of the Roman pantheon having been, ah, borrowed from the Greeks."

One of the boys said angrily, "Father, do we have to stand here and—"

His father interrupted him without compunction. "Continue to enjoy ourselves at this lovely affair? Yes, we do, Naevius, and I'll thank you to keep your mouth shut unless and until you can say something polite."

Naevius turned an unattractive brick red and said no more.

"Gentlemen," a voice said, "I'm so sorry to deprive you of such charming company but there is something urgent requiring the attention of your hostess. Please excuse us.

Tetisheri?" Apollodorus waved his hand in an indeterminate direction and smiled, showing all his teeth.

The two boys blanched. Their father looked as if the statue of Sobek had suddenly come to life.

"Certainly," she said. "Excuse me, gentlemen, it seems I'm needed elsewhere. I hope you enjoy the rest of your evening, and please do bid on the Sobek. He would look very well grouped in with your lares and penates, would he not? And it's always wise to keep a foot in every faith one can. I would think especially one that so predates your own."

Apollodorus took her elbow in an ungentle grip and steered her away.

"What?" she said, all innocence. "A little religious context thrown in at no extra charge. Who could it hurt?"

"You, and Neb," he said grimly. "Not to mention the rest of your family and all your employees and friends."

She wrenched her arm free and glared up at him. "They are beneath our roof and eating our salt."

"The sons especially," he said, "like hogs at a trough. No argument there, but Cassius is a member of the Senate and an acquaintance of Caesar's. It does no one any good to have them insulted in public by a prominent member of a community that at least for now exists primarily on their sufferance."

"And my point is that they should mind their own manners when traveling abroad."

"They don't care," he said, leaning in to speak in a low voice, and the hairs on her neck raised involuntarily at the sensation of his breath on her ear. "They don't have to care. They're Rome."

He was right and she knew it but it still infuriated her. Over his shoulder she saw Uncle Neb looking their way, a fleeting expression of worry on his face—and what was worse, the pearl drooping a little—before he turned to reply to a languid Greek who was trying to gain his attention. Her fury ebbed and was succeeded by a wash of shame. "You're right, of course, Apollodorus." Her eyes drifted toward Cassius and his sons, who had quitted the foul influence of Egyptian gods and were now clustered around the bust of Artemis, who was at least made in their own image, unlike the animal gods of other, inferior races. "I wonder why they stayed," she said. "I would have left."

Another unwelcome face materialized out of the increasingly crowded room. Aurelius Cotta, who smiled when he caught her eye and raised a glass of wine in salute. His eyes became fixed at a point over her shoulder and she turned to see Apollodorus standing a few paces behind her, at his most enigmatic. The two men exchanged a long, expressionless gaze, until a pretty young matron with delusions of seduction claimed Apollodorus' attention. When Tetisheri turned back Cotta had joined Cassius and his sons in obeisance to the progenitor of their Diana.

Really, all the reception was lacking was the presence of Caesar himself and the Roman quorum in Alexandria would be complete in this one room.

She acquired a glass of chilled juice from Nike, who wore

a bright blue silk tunic, sandals that laced to the knee, and a single bracelet above her left elbow with an etching of—yes, the Winged Victory, Nike's namesake. Phoebe must have scoured the marketplace for it. But then anything could be had in the Alexandrian marketplace, for a price. Nike, chin ever elevated, dipped and swayed gracefully through the crowd, offering her tray filled with drinks with a slight graceful bow and a faint regal smile. Naevius snapped his fingers at her but she never seemed to come quite close enough to their part of the room to hear him.

Tetisheri circulated, exchanging pleasantries with Neb's regular customers and introducing herself to the unknowns. She was called upon for information on any number of various items on display and managed to educate without pedantry, an art form she had learned at Neb's knee. Two Egyptian businessmen were exclaiming over two onyx statues of Bast sitting side by side on a marble pedestal, tails curled neatly around their feet.

"It's Bast come to life," one of them said.

"I wonder who the artist is?" The other reached out a hand to the figure on the right, perhaps to pick up the statue and look for the maker's name on the bottom, when the figure came to life, clawed the back of his hand and leaped to the floor to vanish underfoot. The wounded man swore and his friend laughed.

Tetisheri passed on, to intercept that oily old satyr, Nymphodorus, on a clear heading for Keren, who was conversing with three masters from the Library and a group of students who were to a man drooling down the front of her bodice. Tetisheri managed to divert him toward a group of Alexandrian matrons cooing over a display of very fine necklaces, earrings, and bracelets set with rubies, a gemstone that was not often seen this side of Punt. Davos, one of the city's most talented young jewelers, had taken up station over the slabs of white jade like a lion guarding its kill, daring anyone to bid against him.

General Thales came with his wife, Zoe, who greeted Tetisheri fondly, as their daughter had attended some of the same classes at the Mouseion with Tetisheri. Before they moved on Thales said under cover of the noise in the room, "My apologies, Tetisheri. Believe me when I say I would never have allowed the evening to conclude in the manner in which the king had intended." He looked over her shoulder. "But there was no need."

She followed his eyes and saw Apollodorus a short distance away, watching the two of them. "No," she said. "Thankfully not." She didn't know if Thales was telling the truth but she smiled at him and kissed Zoe on the cheek before they moved on. It never profited a trader to hold a grudge, but she made a mental note to add a ten percent handling fee onto anything he might bid on that evening.

Sosigenes arrived late, as usual, and was taken in hand personally by Tetisheri to view the selection of books Uncle Neb had brought back from Berenike which were among the other treasures laid out on the massive display table. These included some fascinating texts in languages that none of them could read. In one, the text was cut into individual pages instead of a single continuous scroll and bound between heavy wooden covers with leather laces, and the progression of the illustrations seemed to indicate the complicated characters arranged in vertical rows should be read from back to front. Well, and Egyptian hieroglyphics could be read in either direction, too, but these characters were drawn with a brush in thick black ink.

"The paper must have been treated with some substance that keeps the ink from bleeding," Sosigenes said, his nose almost touching the page.

Sosigenes had an untidy thatch of dark hair, a long drooping nose and stooped shoulders that made him look far older than he was. His dress at best could be described as rumpled and was entirely unbefitting someone so close to the throne. If he knew he didn't care, and neither, evidently, did the queen. "Fascinating," he said, turning pages with ink-stained fingers she cringed to see touch them, "just fascinating, Tetisheri. The queen would be happy to have this in her private collection, I'm sure."

She raised her eyebrows. "Does that mean you're bidding on it, or that is has just become a generous gift to our most gracious majesty from her most loving subjects?"

He looked up, laughter lighting his angular features. "You know her so well, Tetisheri."

"I do, indeed," she said with a sigh, and went to find Uncle Neb to let him know that one item he had selected for the evening's auction would be withdrawn. He, as he always did, profaned the air with new and inventive curses before bowing to the inevitable. The pearl, however, retained its outraged tilt.

She returned to Sosigenes to report although they both knew the result had been a foregone conclusion. In a voice scarcely above a murmur he said, "And the other business?"

She cast a quick glance around to see if anyone was within earshot. "Nothing to report as yet."

He nodded, and resumed his adoration of the printed matter spread before them. They might even get a sale out of him that evening.

Through it all she felt the continuing regard of Apollodorus, who seemed never to be very far away from whomever she spoke to next. It was unnerving. And, she had to admit, exciting.

Cotta circulated, too, taking care to spend a few moments chatting with every single person there, almost as if he were co-hosting the event. After a while she saw another face she recognized from the previous evening, the long-nosed Greek who had been standing near Linos, Philo, and Thales. He and Naevius and Petronius clustered together, deep in conversation, while Cassius stood nearby with a scowl on his face, all four of them giving the impression they were doing their best not to rub elbows with a room filled with lesser beings.

Naevius tugged at his father's arm and nodded at the door and even from where she stood she saw his father's one-word answer—"No." It must have been very firm because Naevius shrank back, looking thoroughly squelched. And perhaps even frightened? Surely that had to be her imagination. They were staying, even after their unexpected hostess had done her level best to offer insults both implied and overt.

She wondered why. She wondered if she ought to take another try at it.

"Dub," she said, catching his sleeve as he passed, "do you know who that man is? The one with Cassius Longinus and his two sons?"

"Those puppies," Dub said, "they've been to the Five Soldiers frequently since they arrived in Alexandria, and believe me when I tell you you could guarantee a win in any fight if you made their services available to your opponent. Their father at least knows one end of a gladius from the other, but…" He shrugged.

"Yes, but the man with them? The Greek?"

"Him? Oh. Him. That's Polykarpus." She raised her eyebrows and he grinned. "Come, come, Tetisheri, is your memory so short?"

"He looks familiar but I can't place him."

"Polykarpus, my dear Tetisheri, was Arsinoë's closest advisor."

"Of course," she said, "now I remember. How on earth is he still alive? And at large?"

"No idea, although nowadays I hear he has some trouble inhaling, his nose is stuck so far up Ptolemy's ass. Not a position I would enjoy, but we all do what we must to survive, I suppose."

The volume of conversation raised as the levels of wine and beer lowered and the crowd increased to where it spilled out onto Hermes Street. A beaming Uncle Neb called for more lamps. His reception was turning into the social event of the season, and when he caught her eye she smiled and mimed applauding. He looked proud enough to burst, the pearl nearly standing up in salute.

At the Fourteenth Hour, when the crowd had imbibed enough to loosen their purse strings, Neb rang a little bronze bell he had liberated from a dealer in Etruscan antiquities in Rome. "Ladies and gentlemen, lords and ladies, friends, neighbors and visitors from across the Middle Sea, welcome! It is wonderful to see you all here. I hope you've enjoyed yourselves as much as my partner and I—Tetisheri? There you are!—as much as Tetisheri and I have enjoyed having you here. To round off the evening we will be auctioning off just a few of the treasures I brought back from upriver—with a side trip to Berenike, where I assure you, my friends, the wonders of far-off Punt and Sinae are not underrepresented. To prove my point, we'll begin with a lot of white jade, the purest form of that wondrous gemstone. It is translucent enough to capture light and yet still holds up under even the most intricate and elaborate carving. The finest statues, the most delicate jewelry, in all the world jade is unique, of which this, white jade, is the most rare and precious. Now then—"

The white jade went to Davos, who by his expression considered that he'd gotten a bargain. He hadn't, and Tetisheri mentally revised their tax payment upward. A matched set of elephant tusks went to a local shipper known for his fetish for mounting heads, hides, and claws of dead animals on his walls. Tetisheri wouldn't be surprised if in the privacy of his own home he imitated the Pharaohs by draping a leopard skin over his chair, although it would never do to let the queen hear of it. The trappings of royalty remained royalty's prerogative.

Neb's expression was so smug that Tetisheri knew they had paid the expenses for the side trip on this one sale. One of the ruby necklaces went to the matron with the least room for it around her neck, and a beautifully carved sandalwood box filled with peppercorns went for twenty-five times its weight in silver.

Tetisheri helped Uncle Neb sweep the coins into the cashbox and took it to lock away in the office. When she returned to the warehouse, Neb was at the doors, bidding farewell to everyone as they left. She and Aurelius Cotta arrived at the door at the same moment, Cassius and his two sons in tow with Polykarpus trailing behind. "A most successful occasion," Cotta said.

"Thank you, sir," she said. "We're pleased you enjoyed yourself."

He gave her an appraising glance. "Hosted, appropriately, by the most attractive woman in the room."

Her eyes narrowed, and unexpectedly, he grinned. "You are so very easy to vex, Tetisheri. It makes the wish to do so well nigh irresistible."

He made his way out into the darkness, leaving her nothing to say, which was always annoying. And of course the first person to meet her eyes after that was Apollodorus, which was even more so. He did not look happy.

The other three Romans departed in Cotta's wake, Cassius sharing the most minuscule of nods between host and hostess. His sons took no notice of their existence at all, which, given the amount of food and drink they had consumed at Neb and Tetisheri's expense, seemed ungrateful in the extreme. Polykarpus muttered something that might have been thanks but probably wasn't and scuttled out behind them. Tetisheri stared after him.

"Arsinoë's spider," Apollodorus said, and she looked around to find him standing next to her. "All legs and arms and I'll-eat-you-if-I-catch-you purpose."

"How," she said, repeating the question she had asked Dub, "is he still alive and at large? Arsinoë is still in prison in Rome, isn't she? Nobody let her out when I wasn't looking?"

"Oh, she's still in prison, never fear, and scheduled for a prominent place in Caesar's triumph when he returns. Always supposing the Senate allows him to have one."

She stared at him. "Is there any doubt of that?"

He looked down at her. "You're not quite up to speed on politics, are you, Tetisheri?" Without waiting for an answer he went on. "There is a very large faction in Rome who think Caesar is acquiring far too much power far too quickly. A lot of that can be put down to jealousy, obviously, of his abilities and victories and the treasure he has accumulated. Not to mention the pretty impressive collection of queens he has seduced, our own being only the most recent. Speaking of enemies…"

She followed his glance, to where the Romans and the spider were just vanishing between two buildings. "Cassius? I thought he was one of Caesar's allies. And what is he doing here if he isn't?"

"I think the Senate sent him to be their watchdog."

"He was with Caesar at the palace yesterday," Tetisheri said. "Would Caesar really bring an enemy into the queen's presence?"

He looked at her. "Much better your enemy under your nose than behind your back."

"I suppose that's true." Suddenly she yawned so widely tears came to her eyes. It had been a very long day, following on from a very long night.

He smiled. "You're exhausted, and no wonder. What time shall we meet tomorrow to—"

Uncle Neb was closing the big wooden doors. Apollodorus moved to help him. The first floor bolt had dropped when they heard someone call their names. "Wait, please, wait! Apollodorus!"

Apollodorus pushed the door open again and stepped outside. Tetisheri peered around him and saw a man she recognized as one of Aristander's deputies. He was talking rapidly in an undertone. Apollodorus heard him out with a slowly gathering frown. He asked a question. The man answered. Apollodorus nodded and the man rushed off back the way he had come.

"What was all that about?" Uncle Neb frowned at Tetisheri. "A question I seem to be asking often of late."

Apollodorus walked back to the door but ignored Neb's invitation to step inside. Behind Neb and Tetisheri the other four of the Five Soldiers gathered to listen. "Hunefer is dead," Apollodorus said bluntly. "Murdered, on his own doorstep. Tetisheri, you must come with me."

Neb's face darkened. "If you're implying anything, Apollodorus—"

"I'm implying nothing, Neb," Apollodorus said steadily, not looking away from Tetisheri. "You know she'll want you to report back to her on this personally, Tetisheri."

"She?" Uncle Neb said. "Who—" He stumbled to a halt and turned to look at his niece and partner. "Tetisheri—"

"I have to go, Uncle," she said, squeezing his hand. "I'll change and be right with you, Apollodorus."

"Hurry!" he said to her back.

9

*on the First Day of the Third Week
at the Sixteenth Hour...*

Hunefer's house was as close to the palace as it could physically get without actually being on the palace grounds, and there were those who would say—and had—that the exterior ornamentation was the most lavish since Ptolemy Euergertes covered the walls of the Serapeum with the entire history of the cults of Apis and Nemwer and then applied gold leaf to every single figure, including all of the hieroglyphics, of which there were many.

Hunefer's house might not be quite that ornate but it didn't lack ambition. It was completely lacking in taste, however. The main entrance, double doors of gilded cedar, stood ajar, a light flickering from within. As they approached Tetisheri saw Aristander standing on the broad front step with a group of his men. From inside could be heard a woman shrieking. Citizens of Alexandria in their nightclothes under hastily donned cloaks stood in groups of two and three up and down the street, whispering among themselves.

They came to the gate that barred the path to the front doors and in spite of herself Tetisheri's step faltered.

Apollodorus rested his hand on the small of her back, not urging her forward but a simple reminder that she was not alone, that this visit was nothing like the last time she had been beneath this roof. She squared her shoulders, raised her chin in a fair imitation of Nike, and walked through the gate.

Aristander saw them coming and waved them through. His face was grim. "Thank you for coming so quickly, both of you."

"What happened?"

"See for yourself." Aristander stood back.

Hunefer's body was sprawled across his doorstep. His eyes were open and blank, his jaw agape. He'd fallen half on his side, with one arm stretched out, an attempt to touch something now forever out of his reach.

Tetisheri could see no wound. "How—"

Aristander went to stand at Hunefer's head, and turned it. It moved easily. Even in the flickering light of the night watch's torches they could see the dark, ugly wound that matted the hair on the back of his head. There was also some gray, glutinous stuff mingled in the dark strands. Tetisheri, with no cause to have any sympathy for the dead man, still felt nausea tickle the back of her throat. The pungent smells of spilled blood and expelled urine and feces saturated the air. She tried to breathe shallowly through her mouth.

"Struck from behind," Apollodorus said. He and Aristander exchanged a grim look.

Like Khemit, she thought, interpreting that look correctly. She saw that Hunefer was wearing the same sandals he had worn at Ptolemy's court the night before, the ones made of copper links set with carnelians.

I don't know how he managed to walk in sandals so encrusted with gemstones.

In a moment of realization that quite subsumed her nausea, she made a mental note to ask Tarset what kind of gemstones, precisely, encrusted the sandals of the young noble who had visited Khemit's shop. And then she remembered Khemit's weaving. She pointed.

"What?" Apollodorus said.

"His sandals. They look like the ones in Khemit's weaving."

Aristander stood and wiped his hands on a rag one of his men handed to him. "It looks as though they waited until he was on his doorstop with his hand on the latch, and then they rushed him."

"They?"

Aristander shrugged. "They. He. She."

"She?"

"Armed with a club, even a woman could do this." Aristander gave Tetisheri a somber look.

"What the—"

Tetisheri cut off Apollodorus' angry comment with a look. "When did this happen?"

Aristander looked down at the body. "The body has yet to begin to stiffen. Anywhere from one to two hours ago, would be my guess."

"I have been at Uncle Neb's reception, in full view of at least a hundred people, since the Twelfth Hour. Further, I have no reason to kill Hunefer."

"You hated him."

"He hated me and in his opinion with more cause. Sheftu nearly beggared him in the divorce settlement."

Aristander sighed. "I know."

She touched his arm. "It's all right, Aristander. I understand. You had to ask."

Some of the tension eased and he gave a small, apologetic smile. "Like I said. You think like a shurta."

Apollodorus growled something beneath his breath. Tetisheri touched the back of his hand briefly and felt him relax. "May I take a closer look?" he said.

"Of course."

Apollodorus went forward and stooped over the body, his hands searching over Hunefer's scalp. After a few moments he stood up and took the cloth from Aristander's man with a nod of thanks. "The wound is long, thin, and feels to me like it's in a half-circle shape."

"And?"

"Much like a sally stick," Apollodorus said. "Have you seen any similar wounds lately?" Their eyes met and there was a pregnant pause.

"Aristander," Tetisheri said, in a flat, hard tone that made them both look at her. "Take his body to the morgue. Shave his head so you can get a good look at the wound and make a drawing." She hesitated, and added, "You should also shave the heads of any other victims with head wounds who came to your notice recently." They couldn't be more specific with all of Aristander's men standing around.

"And I should do this why?"

"Come here."

Aristander sighed and came to stand next to her. She turned so her back was to the rest of them and reached into her pocket. The Eye of Isis gleamed up at them.

She heard his quick, indrawn breath. He stared from it to her, and even in the dim light she could see the friend warring with the loyal shurta. The friend won. "Are you sure about this?"

She put the Eye away. "It's only temporary."

He raised a skeptical eyebrow, but all impatience vanished from his face and he even bowed his head. "It will be done."

"Send one of your men to my house and bid Keren come to the morgue and do as I asked her."

"Now?"

"Now. Tell your man to tell the morgue attendant she has your full authority."

Aristander gave the order and his man set off at a run. "And now?"

"Is that Ipwet inside?"

While they'd been standing outside the door the shrieking from inside the house had risen and fallen and risen and had now fallen again, replaced by a dull, continuous sobbing. Aristander winced. "That's her."

"Have you talked to her?"

"She found him. She's in no condition to be interviewed."

"Really." It was her turn to be skeptical.

In a lower voice he said, "I know you hate her, and with cause, but she did just lose her son."

"Her son was just murdered. I would think that she'd be interested in finding out who did it."

He cast up his eyes. "Fine, but I'll talk to her, not you."

"Fine," she said. "While you do, Apollodorus and I will search the house."

Aristander looked first startled and then resigned. "As the Eye commands."

"This wasn't a random killing, Aristander. This was a man killed on his own doorstep, and he's still wearing all his jewelry and those ridiculous sandals. And there, look at his belt, he still has his purse. He wasn't robbed. Why, then, was he killed?"

"Just don't let her see you, please?"

They slipped inside through the atrium, bypassing the room where the sobbing was again gaining in volume. Tetisheri led the search in quick, efficient fashion, having far too much familiarity with the floor plan of Hunefer's house.

Like most homes and buildings in Alexandria the house had a single floor and, because the family of Hunefer was old and wealthy when it was built, the rooms were large and well appointed, with tiled floors and walls either paneled in polished wood or painted with murals depicting romantic scenes of rural life featuring farmers and craftsmen. Not that any Hunefer in three generations had ever been closer to a farm than a boat on the Nile. Every wall had its niche and every niche a bust or a statue of a god or an ancestor (that ancestor almost invariably Alexander), the standing lamps were every one of them wrought of the finest bronze, and half a dozen rooms had their own shallow pools, all of which were murky and greening over. There were multiple shrines with candles burning before small figurines carved from ivory and exotic woods. Mostly Greek, of course.

The house had been built more as a showcase than as a place to live in peace and comfort. See how rich and powerful we are, we Hunefers whose line goes back to Alexander. However, compared to Tetisheri's memories of two years before, it now had acquired a slight aura of decay. The coverings on the furniture were threadbare, the paintings on the walls faded, and there were—horrors—cracked tesserae in every room that had not been replaced. A faint layer of dust showed here and there.

"The august House of Hunefer feels down on its luck," Apollodorus said, putting her thoughts into words.

One door was locked and guarded by one of Aristander's men. "The house slaves," he said when they asked.

There was nothing suspect in Ipwet's room other than her ostentatious taste in clothes and furnishings. They came finally to Hunefer's room and Tetisheri had to steel herself before she pushed open the door. Inside, the furnishings were almost exactly the same as when she had left—fled—that dark winter evening, and for a moment she quailed.

"Tetisheri?" His voice was warm, intimate, even, as was his hand, steadying her at the small of her back.

"That night…" She swallowed. "The night I… left this place."

"Yes?"

"He was gambling with Nenwef and others of his friends, and losing. So he placed me as a wager. I was eight months gone with child and I couldn't stand for long, but he paraded me in front of his friends. 'She might be a mongrel but at least she's fertile,' he said. And he laughed. And then they all laughed, too."

She had never told the story before, not to anyone, not to Neb, not to Keren who had attended her labor, never to her mother who had sold Tetisheri into marital slavery in exchange for a connection to one of the oldest and most noble families in Alexandria.

"How did you get away?"

"I said I had to use the chamber pot." Her voice shook. "No matter what my mother said, no matter how angry she was, no matter what she threatened, I would not stay another night in this house." A laugh escaped her that was more a sob. "Although Hunefer's luck was running very badly. Chances were I would have been sleeping somewhere else."

Without any warning, Apollodorus swept her up into a crushing embrace and kissed her, hard, demanding, very nearly ferocious. He forced her mouth open and then licked at her tongue, and his hands were everywhere, cupping her breasts, sliding between her legs to toy with a place she had thought died the day she was married, grasping her hips and pulling her hard against him. He demanded all her focus, all her attention, and he would not be denied.

She shocked herself by rising up on her toes and rocking against him, her legs parting so she felt the full length of him against her, chasing that elusive feeling she had felt only once before when last he kissed her. She heard herself moan, a long, low sound she had never before heard come out of her mouth. He growled and bit the soft spot beneath her ear, sucked at the madly beating pulse at the base of her neck, slid his mouth down to close over the tip of her breast.

She cried out but she did not recoil. In this room where she had suffered so much pain and so many indignities, in this house beneath whose roof she had known only shame and fear, the white heat of his attention and her involuntary response to it seared everything else out of her mind for at least those few precious moments.

He let her go at last and she stood there, staring up at him. They were both breathing hard. She raised her hand and placed it over his heart, and thrilled to the feel of the drumbeat beneath her palm. The same palm he had bitten the night before. It was still a little sensitive. "I thought all that was dead in me," she whispered.

He dropped a light kiss on her mouth. "I was afraid it might be." He smiled. "I'm glad we were both wrong."

She took a deep, shaken breath. "In the meantime, this does not put forward the queen's business."

"Come a time, the queen's business can go hang," he said, his voice still rough with desire.

His retort surprised a laugh out of her, and the laughter stiffened her knees. She turned to look at the room. Now it was just a room, a sleeping room like a thousand others in Alexandria, a room with a wide wooden bed with a light coverlet in dark red, a table bearing a wide onyx bowl and a matching pitcher. A wooden press inlaid with coral and nacre yielded nothing more sinister than Hunefer's clothes, erring always just this side of vulgarity, instead of the elegance to which he and his mother—and her mother—had ever aspired and always failed to achieve.

She even looked under the bed. Nothing.

"There is bound to be an office, with papers."

There was, and a desk piled high with unpaid bills. There were several notices of late payments and one threat to sue if Hunefer did not pay promptly and in full.

"Anything else?"

"The kitchen."

"Do we really think Hunefer even knew where the kitchen was?"

"Let's go look, just in case." She led the way to the back of the house and outside, where the kitchen was housed beneath a roof depending from the edge of the house and two posts. She paused for a long moment.

"What?" he said.

"This was the way I left, that night."

His hand was again warm and reassuring at the small of her back.

The stoves were on the open side, and there was a door into the wall of the house. "Where does that go?"

"The pantry," she said, and opened it. It was dark inside and she groped for the candle she knew was on the shelf to the right of the door. Dinner coals were banked in the stove. She lit a twist of grass from them and touched it to the candle. She went back to the pantry and stepped inside, holding the candle high.

Silence.

"Tetisheri?" Apollodorus came to the door and peered over her shoulder where she had stopped dead. "What—"

The room was small, with shelves piled with herbs and foodstuffs and heavy canvas bags filled with more piled haphazardly on the floor below. Some unlucky slave had dropped a sack of grain and footprints had been left in the residue.

Nothing out of the ordinary so far, nothing to keep Tetisheri mute and frozen. But on the left wall, in a stack that nearly reached the low ceiling, were twenty small wooden chests, sturdily made, each fastened with a hasp and a lock and tightly corded. All but one.

Tetisheri heard Apollodorus swear beneath his breath. She put the candle down on a high shelf, noticing distantly that her hand was surprisingly steady, and went to the chest without the lock. The lid fit tightly around a raised lip and had to be coaxed into opening. When it did, it revealed a thick cloth bag tied tightly at the mouth. "Hold the lid for me, please?"

Apollodorus stepped forward and put his hand on the lid.

She fumbled at the knot and at last pulled it free, and spread the mouth of the bag open. They both stared inside. Finally Tetisheri put in her hand and pulled out a single coin. It felt heavy, and the raised images on the face and back of the coin sharp against her fingertips. She held it closer to the light of the candle. The raised image of Isis and Horus was very clearly stamped into the metal.

It was the same coin Cleopatra had tossed her two days before.

"Get Aristander," she said.

"No," he said. "You go get Aristander and I'll stand guard." He pushed her out of the pantry, shut the door and set his back to it. The gladius at his belt was in his hand.

Aristander came, saw, and summoned more of his men. He ordered all the lamps in the house to be brought out and lit. He opened the unlocked box and called Tetisheri and Apollodorus to witness that, yes, they were looking at what they thought they were looking at. He sent a man to the palace to alert the queen's guard to send a detachment to protect the transfer of an important shipment to the royal treasury as soon as humanly possible.

Tetisheri stood out of the way, watching the chests empty out of the pantry. The remains of the spilled wheat had been obliterated by the tramp of many feet but the grain on the floor beneath the chests was still relatively whole, each of the chests on the bottom row having left behind its own clear, square imprint in the faint dusting. "I need to talk to the cook."

Aristander, organizing the shifting of the chests from the pantry to the street and considerably hampering his own efforts in his determination to have each chest or chests in full view of a minimum of three or more of his men at all times, cast her a harried look. "Fine, yes, go ahead."

She turned on her heel and found the room where the slaves had been sequestered. "Open the door," she told the guard.

He looked over her shoulder. "But Aristander said—"

"He won't be best pleased with you for interrupting him at present. But I'm willing to do it if you are."

He unlocked the door and stood back far enough that no one could blame him if this all went horribly wrong. Tetisheri wrenched open the door and immediately someone inside started wailing.

"Stop that noise this instant," Tetisheri said, in no mood. "Nebet? Nebet, are you in here?" No one had thought to give them a lamp so she couldn't make out individuals in the room's dark interior. Her nose told her that some of them were so terrified they had lost control of their bowels. She pulled back and told the guard in a tone of voice that brooked no denial, "Fetch a lamp and a chamber pot." He hesitated. "Do it. Now."

He scuttled off and she turned back to the room. "Nebet? Please come out here in the hallway where I can see you."

An older, querulous voice answered her out of the huddle

of bodies. "Tetisheri? Is that you? What are you doing back here, child? You know better."

"I really do. Could you come out here, please?"

After a moment Nebet emerged out of the gloom, blinking in the torchlight. "Tetisheri. It really is you. Have you heard? The master is dead."

"Yes, I know."

"They're going to blame us, Tetisheri. The slaves are always blamed."

"I don't think so, Nebet, not this time. I need to ask you a question. When did you last buy grain for the kitchen?"

Nebet was short and wiry, with skin as black as Nike's and muscles like Edeva's on a smaller scale. In two years in this house Tetisheri had had one friend in the one place that afforded her some temporary respite from the hell that was her everyday life. Nebet had not been obliged to offer that respite and indeed had put herself to some not inconsiderable risk by doing so. Rebel called to rebel. There was more gray in Nebet's hair and more lines in her face now but the old defiant fire still burned in her dark eyes. Some people just wouldn't be owned.

She hadn't answered and Tetisheri said again, "When did you last buy wheat, Nebet? Believe me, it's important."

Nebet smiled slowly. "If it's that important..."

In spite of the urgency of the situation Tetisheri had to laugh. "What do you want, my friend? If it's in my power I will give it to you."

"What have I ever wanted?"

Tetisheri considered the cook for a long moment. "Wait here." She went to find Aristander. "I want to remove the cook from this house."

"What the—" He threw up his hands when he saw her hand go to her pocket. "Fine. Of course. Certainly. Anything else I can do? And by all the gods, will you please tell me why?"

"Because I believe she has—unknowingly—information we need." She hesitated. "And, yes, because she's a friend, and I want to help her buy her freedom as soon as possible. Ipwet cannot know, Aristander, because she would forbid water to be boiled ever again if I said I wanted tea."

"Ipwet is not going to be in a position to refuse anything in future," he said grimly, but he accompanied her to the room and Nebet was formally released into Tetisheri's custody.

Tetisheri drew her to one side. "Now tell me. When did you last buy wheat?"

"Yesterday," Nebet said. "And then Gorgo dropped it when she was putting it away in the pantry, the silly little fool, and of course the mistress—" she spat the word "—heard of it immediately and had her beaten, and then Gorgo was too ill to clean up the mess so I had to do it."

And had resented doing something so beneath her station and so had done it badly. "Yesterday," Tetisheri said. "You're sure?"

Nebet looked at her.

"Yes, of course. All right. Thank you, Nebet."

Nebet folded her arms. "Now what?" She was doing her best to sound truculent but there was no mistaking the fear for the future any masterless slave faced in that time and place. Especially one who had died by violence.

Tetisheri's heart turned over. "You'll come home with me."

"For how long?"

"For the rest of your life if you wish, or until you decide what you want to do next."

The calm certainty in her voice pierced Nebet's ironclad composure for the first time. The cook's eyes filled with tears as she allowed herself to believe, perhaps just this once in a life spent in abject service to unkind, unappreciative, and uncaring masters.

Aristander's man hustled up with the chamber pot and the lamp, and the room was revealed to contain six slaves, a quarter the amount that the House of Hunefer had owned when Tetisheri had been in residence. One woman older than Nebet took immediate advantage of the chamber pot. The rest huddled together, fearful of being blamed for the master's death, because slaves were always to blame for something and punished whether they were guilty or not.

"Escort Nebet to my house," she said to Aristander's man. "You know where that is? Good. Nebet, ask for Keren. Say I sent you. She will understand. Go now, and in the name of Isis do not let Ipwet see you."

She was on her way back to the kitchen when she thought of something else. Hunefer's body had, mercifully, been removed from the front doorstep. She caught up with Nebet and the shurta at the gate. "Nebet!"

Nebet turned, the fear that something had gone wrong plain on her face.

"No, no, it's fine, I just need to ask you one more question." Tetisheri caught the cook by the elbow and pushed her across the street and around a corner. The shurta, mystified, brought up the rear.

"What?" Nebet said.

"In the past week, did an older woman come to call? Thin, in her fifties, she would have worn good linens. An air of authority, not deferential at all. She might have asked to speak to Hunefer."

Nebet snorted. "When I'm not at the market I'm in the kitchen. I was not welcome in the front of the house." She paused. "Although—"

"Yes?" Tetisheri said eagerly.

"Now that I think of it, there was a woman such as you describe," Nebet said. "She came round to the back and questioned us about the master."

"What kinds of questions?"

"Where he'd been, what he was doing, who his friends were." She looked at the shurta and leaned forward to whisper in Tetisheri's ear. "She bore the Eye."

"Ah. And you told her—"

Nebet shrugged. "He hosted a dinner for a couple of young Romans and a Greek the week before last. Nothing like the dinners he used to give. I can't remember the last time I made my seafood stew, you know the one with the olives and almonds? Or my lamb in apricot sauce. I—"

"Did you know the names of the guests?"

Nebet shook her head. "As I said. I was never welcome in the front of the house."

It didn't matter. Tetisheri could guess. "You told all this to Khemit, to the woman who was here?"

Nebet nodded. Another thing Tetisheri liked about Nebet was that she never pretended false loyalty to a master she despised.

The shurta escorted Nebet away and Tetisheri crossed to the house and went slowly up the path.

"You."

She looked up to see Ipwet standing in the doorway. The older woman looked nothing like the composed, stylish woman in Ptolemy's throne room the night before. Her face paint had run and dried in streaks, her careful coiffure was tangled beyond repair, and it looked as if she had tried to rend the front of her tunic.

"What are you doing here? Did you come to gloat? Having beggared us, now you come to crow in triumph over the death of a man you always hated? A man you never supported? A man who fathered a child you aborted, even upon the very day of his birth?"

All the rage that Tetisheri had ever felt in a bitter, miserable, agonizing nightmare two years long bubbled up and over. In a voice she barely recognized as her own she said, "The child was stillborn. I did nothing to hasten its death."

"But you hated it!" Ipwet's shriek could have been heard in Rome. "As you hated us! As if you had any right! As if we did not raise you up far beyond your station from that tawdry trade house on the waterfront! Ungrateful, wretched, murderous girl! I curse the day I ever let Hagne into my house to bargain for my son!" She flew at Tetisheri. "I curse you! I call down the curses of all the gods above and below on you and your children and your children's children!"

Tetisheri caught her wrists before Ipwet's nails could rake her face and then Apollodorus was there, seizing the older woman by the waist and lifting her up off her feet. She sagged in his hold, moaning, "Ruined, all in ruins. My son, oh, my son, my son..."

Apollodorus carried her into the house and was back a moment later, grim of face. "Are you done here?"

"Yes," she said. "I'm all done here."

They were ushered into the queen's presence shortly after the First Hour the next morning. Tetisheri, Apollodorus, and Aristander had not slept and the queen looked as if she hadn't, either, although not for the same reason. She kept both hands on her swollen belly as if afraid the child within was going to jump out into the world at his first opportunity. Every now and then she winced, and once Tetisheri thought she saw the imprint of a tiny foot against the thin robe she wore.

"So," Cleopatra said. "My new issue is returned to me. Well done, Tetisheri."

"It was a joint effort, my queen."

The queen looked at Aristander. "And the coin?"

"Is in the strong room in the palace, my queen, under lock and key and with an extra layer of guards around it."

"Good." The baby kicked and the queen took a quick breath.

"A chair, majesty?" Apollodorus said.

She gave him a quick, pained smile. "Thank you, Apollodorus, but at this point it's less comfortable to sit than to stand. He was awake all night. He should sleep soon." She looked at Tetisheri. "Hunefer?"

"The coin was found in his house," Tetisheri said. "And it appears he was in trouble financially."

"But?"

"No buts," Tetisheri said. "This has at least some of the markings of thieves falling out. Stolen coins. A murder at the door of the house where they were hid."

Cleopatra was quick to pick up on what she didn't say. "You believe it was made to look so, rather than actually is?"

Tetisheri spread her hands. "A murder is certain to draw attention. And if he were killed over the coin, why is it still there?"

"You think it has been made to look as if he were involved?"

"Oh, he was involved."

"And?"

"And he was deemed a useful sacrifice when—"

"When what?"

Tetisheri hesitated. "I was going to say, when the thieves

felt us closing in on them." She looked up and met Cleopatra's eyes. "But we weren't."

"Possibly the thieves felt panic at the mere thought of being caught? As well they should have," Cleopatra added with feeling.

"Perhaps."

"But you don't think so."

"My queen." Tetisheri chose her words with care. "You have your coin returned to you, in full. Only one chest was broken into and that we believe is because the thieves wanted to make sure they had stolen what they meant to steal. The new issue is safe in your hands and ready to be released."

Apollodorus glanced at Tetisheri but said nothing.

"The stolen coin was found in the house of Hunefer," Tetisheri said, "who himself was found dead on his own doorstep."

Cleopatra's mouth tightened.

"You have your stolen property recovered, and you have the house it was found in, and you have the man who owned the house, dead, true, but when alive it is obvious he was in serious financial difficulties. The bills we found in his office confirm that, as I'm sure his mother will when questioned."

"What is your point, Tetisheri?"

Tetisheri spread her hands. "This investigation could stop here, majesty. You have the stolen property, found in the home of a very likely suspect. It is unfortunate that he cannot be questioned, but the circumstances could be construed as being self-evident by all but the most critical observer."

"But you don't think he did this alone."

"I know he didn't, majesty," Tetisheri said firmly. It was, in fact, the one thing of which she was absolutely certain.

"Why not?"

"Because, majesty, I knew Hunefer only too well. It would have been impossible for him to construct such a perfect plan, let alone execute it so efficiently." She paused. "I don't think he would even have had the capacity to think of it in the first place as a means to alleviate his monetary problems. He just wasn't that intelligent."

A faint smile crossed Cleopatra's face and her hands dropped from her belly. "I'll take that chair now, Apollodorus."

He pulled a chair out and the queen subsided into it with care. "So you think he had a partner or partners, and that they are still at large."

Tetisheri hesitated for a long moment. The queen seemed willing to wait for her answer until Ra set again in the west. "I do," Tetisheri said at last. "There have been two murders, remember, both committed the same way with the same weapon."

Cleopatra raised her eyebrows.

"A sally rod, majesty," Apollodorus said. "A long, thin, round rod made often of willow but occasionally of other, more durable woods. Army sergeants often carry them to, er, enforce discipline during training. It would be all too easy to lay hands on one."

"Such a weapon could kill?"

"Made from a hard enough wood, wielded with enough force? Yes. Especially if the killer knew what he was doing."

"And this one did," Aristander said. He was in no mood to betray Maat and let killers walk free in a city he considered as much under his protection as it was Cleopatra's. "We shaved the heads of both Hunefer and Khemit. The wounds are nearly identical, and almost identically placed. They were much of a height and were killed with the same weapon, most likely by the same person." He glanced at Tetisheri. "This is the conclusion of my own coroner, as well as that of an independent authority brought in to consult."

"And, majesty, there is the fact that the coin itself had been moved to Hunefer's pantry only last night." Tetisheri thought. "Well, night before last now."

All three of them stared at her. "And how do you come to this extraordinary conclusion?" Aristander said, forgetting himself enough to speak before and without permission from his sovereign.

Apollodorus snapped his fingers. "The grain."

Tetisheri nodded. "The cook bought it the day before yesterday, and one of the kitchen slaves dropped a sack as she was moving it into the pantry. There was still some on the floor. When Aristander's men took the chests out, you could see their outlines in the grain.

"The coin was stolen eight days ago. To hold it safe, where none of us heard a whisper of its location, and then move it to Hunefer's house one night before he is killed on his own doorstep?" She shook her head. "A reckless move indeed, and one fraught with peril for the thieves. Hunefer was not beloved by his slaves. They would have talked of the chests in the marketplace and the news would have been all over the city in a day. No." She shook her head. "The movement of the chests and Hunefer's murder were concomitant. The perpetrator wanted him associated with the theft and his mouth permanently shut so he couldn't deny it."

A long silence.

"So." Cleopatra sat long in silence, staring over their heads, one hand caressing her belly now rather than rubbing it. They waited. Tetisheri felt a wave of exhaustion and swayed a little where she stood. Apollodorus' hand reappeared, warm and steadying at her back. Tetisheri leaned into it, just a little, but she was sure the queen saw anyway. She made no comment, however, for which Tetisheri was profoundly grateful.

"Well," Cleopatra said, placing her hands on the arms of her chair and sitting upright. The uraeus Ptolemy had worn so carelessly two nights before was on her brow in spirit, cold, gold, and deadly. "Do you have any avenues of inquiry that you feel might be productive to follow?"

"One at least, majesty," Tetisheri said, "and possibly two."

"Then follow them, Tetisheri. I want their names." The queen leaned forward, her eyes hard. "All of their names, everyone who was involved in this conspiracy to rob my kingdom. I don't care who they are. Bring them to me."

"Majesty." Tetisheri bowed her head.

They had managed to enter the palace unseen by any but Cleopatra's personal guards. Their exit was not so discreet. Tetisheri walked into the atrium, only one door away from the street, there to be confronted by Aurelius Cotta, wide awake and offensively cheerful. He was, mercifully, alone, because Tetisheri didn't have it in her that morning to duel with Caesar, too.

"Ah, Tetisheri." He clasped her hand warmly before she could move it out of reach. "Many congratulations on the successful conclusion of your investigation."

She felt Apollodorus and Aristander stiffen behind her. She herself didn't know what to say. If she thanked him, she would be admitting there was an investigation, and if she didn't, he might be alerted to the fact that it wasn't concluded. "Aurelius Cotta," she said. "You are an early riser."

He gave her a sunny smile. "It has always been my motto that the one to greet Apollo as he begins his day's journey is the one most likely to receive the news first. Good and bad, and I'm delighted that he carries good news in his chariot this morning. The queen must be so pleased with you." He allowed his face to fall into lugubrious lines and shook his head. "Although such a shame about the young man, wasn't it? Such a noble house, and for its son to fall so far as theft, and from his own sovereign, too." He waggled a finger. "Hear me, because I speak from personal observation: his family will never recover. Yes, yes, it is true, such things happen even in Rome, as unbelievable as that may sound." He grew stern. "An object lesson to other youths who might be tempted from the path of virtue and probity."

"Tell me, Aurelius Cotta," Tetisheri said, "have you ever thought of taking to the stage?"

He laughed. It even sounded genuine. "Congratulations again, Tetisheri. By the way, I enjoyed myself very much at your reception last night. Your catalogue is impressive. I don't wonder at your enjoyment of your work. I'm sure you'll be very happy indeed to get back to it."

He kissed the back of her hand before she could prevent it, nodded at both men, and strode off.

She turned to stare as he passed out of sight. His hints could not have been broader and she would have to have been very stupid indeed not to interpret them correctly. The investigation had come to a successful conclusion and she was to return to her life and give the theft—and the thieves—no more of her attention.

She remembered the scene in Ptolemy's throne room and in her mind she went around the circle of advisors, royal favorites, august visitors, and court sycophants again, lingering here and there.

All of their names, everyone who was involved in this conspiracy to rob my kingdom. I don't care who they are.

She turned to Aristander. "Release Laogonus' crew and tell them to report directly to their ship."

She looked at Apollodorus. "Go to Laogonus and tell him we sail for Lemesos as soon as you and I and the crew are on board."

10

A brisk following wind carried them to Cyprus in a little over two days but it might as well have been two years for Tetisheri, who saw a pirate sail in every wisp of cloud on the horizon. To exist at the mercy of the wind seemed to her to be almost suicidally reckless. And yet, Cleopatra had tasked these men and this ship with her most confidential missions. There was some mystery here, if only she could forget that they were traveling under the threat of eminent doom.

Debu let out a line and the wind filled more of the single sail, causing it to belly out over the port side. The *Thalassa* heeled more sharply to port. With a dismayed squeak Tetisheri caught hold of the nearest object, which that time happened to be Apollodorus. "Calm down," he said, which she might have forgiven if he hadn't been grinning, too.

"Calm down, the man says," she said bitterly. "Calm down, when at any moment the wind could die and we could be overtaken and attacked by pirates from Oea to Rhinoccorua."

"Really," he said, still grinning. "I had no idea word of our presence spread so far."

"Go ahead, laugh," she said, and clutched him again when Debu let out a little more line and the *Thalassa* heeled even more perilously to port. "Look at that, the water is nearly over the side!"

"But see how much faster we are moving than we would be under the old square sail," he said, pointing at their stern.

She had to admit, if only to herself, that they were leaving a boil of a wake behind them. A dark speck on the horizon caught her eye. "Look! What's that? There, you see? Is it a ship?"

"No, I believe that might be a cormorant."

A moment later the shape resolved into a large pair of wings beating against the sky.

A dark shape surfaced to starboard. "That!" she said, pointing. "What's that? Is that a ship?"

"No, I think that is a school of dolphins."

The sail flapped and she regarded it anxiously. "Is the wind failing?"

Debu tightened the line. The sail filled again and the *Thalassa* leaped forward.

"What I wouldn't give for twenty strong oarsmen," she said. Possibly she growled. She didn't get a wink of sleep during the entire journey and she greeted the shoreline of

Cyprus with inexpressible relief.

"Yes, yes, hilarious," she said tartly when the crew laughed at her, again. "I imagine you'll find it a tad less amusing when we're boarded by the Brundisi and sold into slavery on the return trip. Those of us who are not slaughtered out of hand." The deck rose suddenly beneath her feet and she clutched at Apollodorus. She looked up and saw an expression cross his face that she didn't recognize. "What?"

The expression was gone as if it had never been, and he smiled at her. "Why," he said, his voice a silky purr that reminded her of Bast at her most duplicitous, "only that it would please me very much indeed to encounter the pirates of Brundisium. It is said they are very efficient. But not, as I understand it, entirely reliable."

Her jaw dropped. "Reliable," she said. "Reliable?"

Apollodorus and Laogonus and Debu and Pert and Leon and Bolgios looked at each other and laughed uproariously, and she could only shake her head in disbelief. "The queen employs madmen on her most important business. Certainly someone should tell her."

"Oh, she knows," Laogonus said, his teeth white against his beard, and they all laughed and laughed.

"Madmen," she said with conviction.

The agent's second-in-command, a short, thin Greek with thick, dark, badly cut hair and delicate hands, had been visibly vibrating with anxiety since first sight of the Eye. Tetisheri made a soothing gesture. "Peace," she said. "If you are innocent of any complicity in this crime you have nothing to fear."

He wasn't a slave, he was a freedman, but there was an excellent chance he would be interrogated anyway, and harshly because as they both knew the Shurta had been beating confessions out of the guilty and innocent alike for four thousand years. There was an even better chance that he would be demoted and possibly out of a job entirely, and they both knew that, too. "Here, sit down, Gelo. Apollodorus, some wine, please." She waited as the freedman gulped it down. "Tell me about the coins. When did the order for them come?"

"When we received the dies."

When he said nothing further she said, "And that was…?"

"The first month of Shemu," he said obediently. "I think the Second Week."

"Do the dies always come from Alexandria?"

He nodded. "They are always designed and cut by the Royal Coiner in Alexandria. We create molds from the dies, smelt the bronze, and stamp out the coins here, and then ship them to Alexandria."

The Ptolemys' coins had always been made on Cyprus because copper and tin were plentiful there and because there was wood for fuel. "Who knew about the order?"

"Paulinos. Myself. Harmon, the master of the workshop, because he makes them, and the men who work for him."

"How many employees does he have?"

"Twenty men—smelters, punchers, strikers, and engravers."

"Have there been any changes in personnel recently? Anyone quit due to a grievance?"

He shook his head and said vehemently, "No. Nothing. We are all of us freedmen and well paid. Most of us are married with children and homes. We have too much to lose to engage in theft." His lip actually curled on the word.

Like Laogonus and his crew, Tetisheri thought. The queen made sure those essential to the realm had too much to lose to be tempted into betrayal.

"And the carrier who took the coins from the forge to the port?"

"Almost always the same company and has been for years. And they are always accompanied by the same guards so that nothing happens between the forge and the ship."

"Almost always?"

"Oh." He was relaxed enough now to roll his eyes. "Last year a new carrier convinced Paulinos to give them a try. They'd imported some camels from Jaffa. It was a disaster." He made a face. "They may be great in the desert but the island is better suited to donkeys."

"Where is Paulinos?"

"He hasn't been in all week. The news of the theft hit him pretty hard."

"How did that news arrive and when?"

"A messenger from Alexandria, on..." His eyes narrowed

in thought. "The Eighth Day? No, the Seventh Day. Of the Second Week."

The same day Khemit had received a visitor in her shop. "We have to find Atet upon our return," she said to Apollodorus.

"We do," he said. "Gelo, did this messenger have a name?"

Gelo shook his head. "As soon as Paulinos saw him the two of them left together."

"What did he look like?"

"I only saw him from a distance. I got the impression of a thin, dark man." He considered. "With a very long nose that drooped at the end. Like a flamingo's."

Polykarpus. "And Paulinos has not been back to the shop since?"

"No."

"Is that normal for him?"

Gelo looked puzzled. "Why, I—well, no, I suppose it isn't. He takes weeks off occasionally but he always tells us when he won't be in, and of course he never does when we have a new issue in process. None of us do."

Tetisheri exchanged a glance with Apollodorus, who said, "Take us to his home. Now."

Paulinos lived in a stuccoed villa overlooking the town, with a terrace along the front, a small, well-tended garden at the side, and six tiers of grape vines that climbed the hill behind the house. It was reached by a series of trails connected by flights of stairs switching back and forth on the face of the hillside. There were no houses built above his.

"Idyllic," Apollodorus said.

Tetisheri climbed the last few steps to the terrace and paused to catch her breath. "He has to be in good health."

Gelo, puffing along in the rear, said between gasps, "He says he doesn't like being bothered."

"Is he married?"

"He was. She died last year."

"Any children?"

"One, a daughter, in Rome. Sent to live with a cousin, I think he said. After his wife died. The door's around this way."

They followed him around through the garden, where a patch of seedlings were wilting by the row and even the leaves of the rosemary bush were curling. Gelo paused. "That's odd. Paulinos loved his garden. Why would he—"

His head turned as Tetisheri went swiftly past him with Apollodorus hard on her heels.

The door stood slightly ajar and the smell hit them well before they reached the source of it. Tetisheri looked at Apollodorus with wide eyes and he gave a grim nod. "Wait outside, Gelo," he said.

"Why? What's wrong? I—" And then the smell hit him, too, and his face went white and he turned to vomit into the hedge of verbena that lined the walkway. Well, Tetisheri thought, trying not to follow suit, it needed watering like everything else.

Apollodorus pushed the door wide. "Wait here," he said,

and went in. She heard the dull thuds of shutters being thrown wide and other doors opening. Apollodorus reappeared with a corner of his cloak held to his nose. "I'm sorry, Sheri, but you need to see this."

"See what?" Gelo said. "Is it Paulinos? Is he—"

"Paulinos is dead," Apollodorus said, "and for some time now." He disappeared back inside and Tetisheri stiffened her spine and followed him.

It was a small house, perfectly proportioned, with no atrium, just one long room with the wall facing seawards made of a row of windows with sills wide enough to sit on. The view of the town and harbor of Lemesos was panoramic and spectacular. In the back were two bedrooms. The bathroom between them had a hypocaust to heat the water and a bronze strigil hanging from an ornate hook on the wall next to the bath. A man Tetisheri assumed to be Paulinos was in the bath, and although his flesh had darkened and collapsed onto his bones it was obvious how he had died. His left wrist had been sliced open to the bone, which gleamed white between the curled-back lips of severed flesh. His right hand was lying on the tile, a dagger next to it. The cut wrist was in the water in which Paulinos was reclining and the blood from it had colored the water a dull pink.

Tetisheri swallowed hard. "How long, do you think?"

Apollodorus picked up the dead man's right hand and let it fall. It dropped loosely, smacking into the tiles. "It has been long enough for the death stiffness to wear off, and for the rot to set in. And for the flies to lay eggs."

Paulinos' mouth was open in a soundless scream and the flesh of his face seemed to move, as if he would say more, until Tetisheri realized it was the maggots eating the soft tissue. She bolted from the bathroom into the living room and leaned out of the first open window and gripped the sill. There was a cool breeze off the sea and it felt wonderful on her hot face. After a few moments she had the nausea under control and turned back to the room.

Apollodorus had followed her and was waiting. "I'm sorry," he said again.

"No. You were right. I had to see." She took a deep breath, still breathing shallowly through her mouth, although the smell in the living room was mercifully weaker than in the room where the body lay. "What else is there?"

In the main room two long couches faced each other with a low table between them. The table held a lamp, a carafe, and two cups. There was also a small brazier, the coals long dead. It held a charred curl of papyrus that surprisingly didn't disintegrate when Tetisheri plucked it out. Very carefully she flattened the papyrus and Apollodorus came to look over her shoulder.

"—I—N—A," she spelled out. "Ina?"

"Perhaps Paulina," Gelo said from behind them. "His daughter. The one in Rome?"

"Why write down her name and then burn it?" Tetisheri said.

Gelo peered over her shoulder. "Oh, that isn't his writing."

They both looked at him. "Are you sure?" Tetisheri said.

"Y-yes," he said, his fear returning at the sharpness of her tone. "He and I and Harmon can all write. It's necessary for the job. Every step of the process must be recorded for our report back to Alexandria. I know his hand like I know my own."

"Whose writing is it, then?" Tetisheri said.

He nearly wet himself. "I don't know! It isn't mine! You can ask Harmon, he'll tell you! I never saw this hand before!"

"Calm down." Apollodorus was as exasperated as Tetisheri was with Gelo's histrionics. "No one has offered you harm." The *yet* was unspoken but understood.

Gelo sniffed and gulped and heaved out a shuddering sigh, and then fell into a coughing fit as the smell of the decaying corpse hit his nostrils again. He looked over his shoulder at the bath. "Is he in there?"

"I told you to wait outside," Apollodorus said.

Gelo hesitated, and in his face Tetisheri could see relief that it wasn't him, not this time, along with a natural curiosity to look on the face of death.

"Go," Apollodorus said, his deep voice implacable.

There was no gainsaying that order. Gelo went, unwillingly, but he went.

"The bedrooms," Tetisheri said. They searched them and found nothing. The lean-to on the back of the house that was the kitchen yielded no information, either, other than that it looked like Paulinos had been cooking for himself, and not well. They met again in the living room.

"This house hasn't been cleaned in a while," Tetisheri said. "Dust in the corners, cobwebs in the windows, the covers on the bed look like they haven't been washed in a month. Did the man have no slaves?"

"Gelo said his wife died last year," Apollodorus said. "He may have sold them after his daughter left for Rome. A lot of men don't know how to manage after they lose a spouse."

Tetisheri looked at the table. "Two cups indicates two drinkers. Does the body look like Paulinos might have killed himself on the same day he received the visitor from Alexandria?"

"I'm no doctor but I've watched enough people die and seen more than my share of their bodies afterward," Apollodorus said. "Given the condition of the corpse, I would guess his visitor could actually have watched him die."

Tetisheri looked at the curl of papyrus she still held. "What can I put this in that will keep it safe until we get home?"

They rummaged about in the kitchen and found a small clay jar with a stopper used for dried thyme. Tetisheri emptied it and packed the scrap of papyrus in straw and sealed the stopper with wax. They quit the house with relief.

Gelo was waiting for them on the walkway, the sour smell of his vomit still faint on the air. He was looking at the house with a speculative expression, almost as if he were measuring the windows for curtains. "Does the house come with the job?" Tetisheri said.

He flushed. "Uh, well, yes, it does."

"Congratulations," Apollodorus said.

Gelo, totally missing the sarcasm, actually made a small bow. "Thank you. It is a very nice house. Paulinos Longinus—poor man, we shall miss him—Paulinos Longinus was very happy here. At least until his wife died. He seemed to fall apart after that, poor—"

"Paulinos Longinus?" Tetisheri said.

Gelo looked taken aback. "That was his name."

"Paulinos *Longinus*?"

Mystified, Gelo said, "Paulinos Longinus was his full name, lady. Have I not said so?"

"Not soon enough," Tetisheri said, and turned to Apollodorus. "We have to go."

"Now?"

"Right now." She turned on her heel and headed for the path down the hill. Her feet slipped on loose dirt and pebbles but she took the corners as if she were entered in the pankration at Olympia.

Gelo, panting along in the rear, said, "Wait, aren't you going to report this to the local authorities?"

"No time," Tetisheri said.

"But what will I tell them?" His wail made him sound like a frightened child.

"Whatever you like!"

Behind her Apollodorus said, "Tell them a report will come from the Shurta in Alexandria."

"But when?"

"When one is written!"

11

on the Eighth Day of the Third Week
at the Second Hour...

The first day of their journey back to Alexandria the *Thalassa* had skated across the top of the Middle Sea like an eagle, its sail swung out at a right angle to the ship. It took everything Laogonus had to hold the tiller on course, and at that one of the crew and Apollodorus had to spell him every other hour.

"No wonder you don't need oars!" Tetisheri had said, wiping the spray from her eyes. In spite of her forebodings, she was beginning to enjoy this mode of travel.

His teeth bared in his perpetual grin, the captain laughed. "Poseidon is with us this day!"

Poseidon, however, could be a fickle god, and he deserted them altogether on the second day. The wind faltered at the Sixth Hour and failed them entirely by the Eighth. There was no cloud from horizon to horizon and Ra was merciless as he shone down on a sea that reflected their own faces back at them in perfect detail when they looked over the side.

"Perfect weather for pirates," Laogonus said.

He didn't appear anywhere near as worried at the prospect as Tetisheri thought he ought to be. She felt like the target in the sand pit in the back of the Five Soldiers. Insubstantial zephyrs danced tantalizingly around the ship to the point that she began to take it personally, and to wonder just whose side Poseidon was on. She gripped the amulet of Bast hung round her throat but cats were notoriously averse to water so there would be no help from that quarter.

It helped, a little, that she couldn't stop thinking about the theft and all the things they had discovered related to it over the past week. She wanted, she needed, it was almost a physical necessity to get back to Alexandria to apprise the queen of their findings, and to apprehend the rest of the thieves and the murderer and bring them to justice. She paced up and down the deck as if that might bring her closer to their destination. In truth the water looked flat enough to walk upon and hard enough to bear her weight.

Her perambulations followed a somewhat less than a straight line, by necessity forced to avoid the large piece of equipment in the center of the ship hidden beneath a lashed tarp. No one had bothered to explain what it was. Certainly there was no such thing on board Uncle Neb's *Hapi*. Although the *Hapi* did have oarsmen, seven a side, and this afternoon *Thalassa*'s lack of them felt injudicious in the extreme.

Apollodorus joined her on her tenth trip to the bow. "Longinus?" he said.

"Who else do we know who shares that family name?"

He was silent for a full length of the ship. "*Skatos*," he said. "Cassius. The man who was with Cotta and Caesar the morning I fetched you to the queen's presence."

"Exactly."

"And he was at the kinglet's dinner party that evening," he said slowly. "Sitting at Ptolemy Theos' right hand, too. His guest of honor."

"With his two sons," she said. "And on the other side of the Longinus family was…"

He stopped pacing, and she turned to watch his expression change. "Hunefer."

"Exactly." She resumed pacing, only to stub her toe on the piece of equipment sitting beneath the lashed tarp for the third—or was it the fourth?—time. "Ouch! What is this thing, anyway, and why does it have to be right in the middle of where I'm walking?"

"Temper," he said mildly.

She gave him an unfriendly look and started pacing again, this time with the addition of a slight limp. "We have Paulinos Longinus in charge of making coin for Alexandria and Egypt. We have Cassius Longinus in Caesar's train but dining with Cleopatra's brother and sworn enemy, in company with an Alexandrian noble family known for its allegiance to Ptolemy and not coincidentally in financial trouble of its own."

"More for its hatred of Cleopatra," he said. "What did she do to them, anyway?"

"They backed Arsinoë in the late rebellion," she said, and this time she stopped. "Polykarpus. He was the fourth man in the group of Ptolemy's advisors, with Linos, Thales, and Philo, remember? And Philo is known to be the head of the faction of nobles that most vehemently opposes Cleopatra's rule. The Alexandrian nobles resented the tax levy last year, in spite of her summoning all of them to that conclave to explain why they were necessary. They live their lives in Alexandria, they raise their children there, the whole world visits and trades and studies there, you'd think they'd want the sewers to work properly."

"It's not about the sewers," Apollodorus said. "They're afraid she's going to spend all their money on books for the Library, in particular books to replace the ones that were lost in the fire when Caesar burned his ships."

"Why would they think that?"

"Because someone has been saying it, repeatedly, in marketplaces and tavernas and in every wealthy home within and without the walls of Alexandria ever since she levied the tax."

"Rumor," she said.

"Repeated often enough, rumor begins to look like fact."

"You think it's deliberate?"

"It is too convenient a rumor for her enemies. Put that together with the influence Caesar would appear to have over the queen and it's no wonder more nobles are drifting toward Ptolemy. He called her a mongrel openly in front of a room full of people guaranteed to spread such an epithet from Thebes to Rome. Many of the old houses feel the same, that Auletes foisted a blood usurper in Arsinoë's place. Arsinoë, you will remember, being the true blood daughter of Auletes and his sister. Which so far as I could tell was the only reason to support her, for the uraeus never sat on a head with fewer brains inside it, and, yes, I include the kinglet in that assessment."

She frowned at him. "But the nobles are almost unanimously in favor of this alliance with Rome. We give them grain and gold and they protect us and leave us alone to rule ourselves. Mostly."

"Caesar has got their queen big with his child. It seems obvious to them that Rome's influence will always lean Cleopatra's way. They're for Caesar only so long as she is not at his side."

"But Ptolemy is such a spoiled, willful child," she said. "He doesn't know how to build anything, he only knows how to break things. Can they not see that?"

"'No one loves the messenger who brings bad news.'" He sighed. "Sophocles and his annoying ability to have the proper epigram for every occasion aside, you know full well the Alexandrians and the Greeks in particular dislike Cleopatra's determination to give the Egyptians a strong presence in the kingdom. Remember all the rumblings when she escorted the new bull to the temple in Baucis? I don't think one Greek Alexandrian noble family was in attendance."

She ran through the faces that crowded her memory of the event and had to concede that he was correct.

"As for Polykarpus, a dangerous man, that," Apollodorus said thoughtfully. "He managed to chase Cleopatra out of Alexandria to seek refuge upriver and keep Arsinoë's backside on the throne for almost a full year. I wouldn't have put a single drachma on her staying on the throne a week. It certainly wasn't her doing."

"What was he before he was Arsinoë's advisor? Do we know anything about his background?"

"I think we'd rather know something about his life now," Apollodorus said dryly.

She stopped in her pacing and faced him. "What I want to know is if he ever trained as a soldier. And if so, if he has killed in action, and with what weapon."

"As, for example, a sally rod."

"Exactly."

"You are good at this."

She looked up, startled, to meet his eyes. The twinkle that usually lurked there was in abeyance for the moment. "You always seem to know the right question that should be asked to move the investigation along," he said. "It's a gift given to very few, Tetisheri, but you have it."

"Sail ho!"

They both looked up to see Debu sitting on the masthead, staring to starboard.

They turned as one and squinted into the west, and there, clearly outlined by Ra's pitiless rays, was a single mast growing taller on the horizon. A hull soon rose beneath it, and oars that dipped into the water at the beat of a drum.

"Pirates," Tetisheri said in a hollow tone.

"Pirates," Apollodorus said, a queer sort of smile on his face.

She glared at him. "Now would be a good time to break out the oars. Oh, wait, we don't have an oars, do we?"

"Pirates!" Laogonus whooped out the word and Tetisheri stared incredulously as he threw back his head and laughed. "Now we shall see some fun!"

"'Fun'?" she said. "Did he say 'fun'?"

Apollodorus gripped her shoulder, forcing her to look up at him. "Do you have a knife?"

"Always," she said.

"Good." He said nothing more but he didn't have to. She knew full well what would happen to her if the ship fell into pirate hands.

The crew exploded into action. Debu leaped to the mysterious object at center line and began whipping the lines free. The others formed a supply line from deck to hold and began passing objects up. They looked like—

"Amphora?" Tetisheri said blankly. "Is this really a moment for olive oil? Are we just going to grease the ship so they slide off when they try to board?"

"Not olive oil," Debu said, his lips pulled back in a savage grin as he stripped away the tarp to reveal a ballista bolted securely to the deck.

Tetisheri's jaw dropped. "What—what—"

"Can you shoot?"

She turned to see Old Pert holding out two recurved bows with two quivers full of arrows tipped with broad, flat bronze heads. "Yes, she can," Apollodorus said, and Tetisheri transferred her incredulous gaze to him. "Pirates don't wear armor as it will take them to the bottom if they fall overboard, so a direct hit with one of these should disable or kill." He grinned at her, and to her steadily growing indignation she saw that he, like Laogonus, like the rest of the crew, seemed actually to be enjoying the prospect of this encounter. While she, for her part, was wondering exactly and precisely where to place her knife so as to not be raped to death.

He bent the string onto first one bow and then the other. He gave her one. "Try a dropping shot first, to—"

"Yes, yes, to get the range," Tetisheri said testily. "I remember that much from the lessons at the Five Soldiers." She took the bow, held it in her left hand and drew on the bowstring with her right. A tiny bump of wood had been fixed to the limb just above the grip for use as a sight, and she used it to aim at the pirate ship, which was closing with them at alarming speed.

She heard a grunt and a grinding sound and looked around to see that one of the amphoras had been placed on the slider of the ballista. The amphora had an unusually large mouth with a piece of hide stretched across it. Beneath the outwardly curved lip of the mouth was a line of tightly tied twine, securing the hide so that there was no leakage from within.

She was beginning to understand. "What is inside them?"

Laogonus' grin was savage. "Let's let the pirates answer that, shall we? Don't fire until I give the signal, do you hear?"

Assent came from the crew, one of whom stood by to help load the ballista. The other three lined the rail, armed with bows like Tetisheri and Apollodorus.

First sighted a league distant, the ship had closed to half a league while they armed themselves. The boom of the drum from the other ship was getting louder and the details of the pirates' ship were much more clear. She bore no name and no flag and she looked old enough to have ferried Hannibal's elephants from Africa to Italy.

A quarter of a league and they could hear the slice of the oars into the water. A tenth of a league and she could distinguish the faces of the pirates. A rough count totaled about twenty in all, not including the rowers who were probably chained in place. Some cool part of her brain noticed that they looked a miserable lot, ragged, filthy, emaciated. They were hungry, which meant they wouldn't give up this prize without a fight.

For the first time in her life Tetisheri prepared herself to shoot to kill. Her mouth went dry, and she had to blink the sweat out of her eyes.

Closer they came, closer. Clearly audible to the crew of the *Thalassa*, the order rang out on the other ship to raise oars on the port side. They did so and drifted ever nearer. As one Tetisheri and the rest notched their arrows and drew back on their bowstrings, lining up on either side of the ballista. It was as yet hidden from the pirates' view.

The pirate crew sneered and yelled insults and obscenities.

One turned and raised his tunic to show them his naked and extremely hairy backside. It was not an edifying sight, and yet for some reason the action steadied Tetisheri's nerves. The fine tremor along her arms ceased and she sighted along the arrow to a little above the pirate who had so aptly demonstrated that he wasn't wearing a clout.

"Wait," Laogonus said, almost crooning the word, "wait…"

The pirates stood on the railing, preparing to jump to the *Thalassa* when they were within range.

There was a tremendous *THWAAAANG* from behind her and one of the huge pottery jars flew over the side of the *Thalassa* and landed squarely on the center deck of the pirate ship. Artemis herself could not have aimed it better. The jar shattered on impact and sent a white cloud of some powdered substance up into the air like a miniature cloud. The pirate ship was still making way and the rear half of the ship was dragged inexorably through it. The pirates who breathed in the powder were immediately affected, coughing, choking, clawing at their noses and throats. Their faces turned bright red and they began dropping to their knees, and then falling prone, their heels drumming on the deck.

The sounds from the pirate ship were excruciating to listen to and Tetisheri was almost glad when Laogonus shouted, "Fire!"

As she loosed her bowstring she heard the thud of another projectile being loaded into the ballista, followed by the rough scrape of wood against wood, all the while she was shooting as fast as she could pull another arrow from her quiver and sight down its length. Her first shot found the mast of the other ship, her second narrowly missed the pirate who wasn't wearing anything beneath his tunic, her third caught the man next to him in his left eye. She drew back on her fourth shot as another *THWAAAANG* sounded behind her and another jar flew overhead and again hit the pirate ship, this time just aft of the bow. Momentum kept the pirate ship moving and the *Thalassa* slid astern, and looking up the length of the other ship's deck they could plainly see the hundreds of spiders and scorpions scuttling across the deck in the wreckage of the jar. The pirates were shouting and screaming and there were splashes as some jumped overboard. The oarsmen began to scream, too, when the spiders and scorpions overran the well in which they were chained.

Poor wretches, she thought, sickened. She clenched her teeth and set another arrow to her bow. It sang in her ear and caught a man in the back. He arched, his hand reached behind him, clawing for it, and then he fell forward out of her sight. Next to her Apollodorus' bow spoke and another pirate fell with an arrow buried in his heart.

The pirates were desperate and one who appeared to be the captain whipped those oarsmen who weren't bitten or asphyxiated into putting their oars back in the water. The ship turned, a little unsteadily, and came back at them for another pass. Laogonus waited until they were in range and *THWAAAANG* went the ballista again. This time a ball of snakes rolled out of the pottery shards, cobras, most of them, or so it looked from where Tetisheri watched, horror-struck.

The screams of the pirates and the oarsmen intensified and more splashes were heard. The oars lost rhythm and clashed and tangled with each other. The ship lost way, slowed and in very short order stopped, dead in the water.

Tetisheri, breathing hard, lowered her bow and stepped back from the railing. Her entire body was suddenly possessed of a fine inner trembling. She made her way to the bow on unsteady feet and sat down hard on the deck, still holding her bow.

"Are you all right?" Apollodorus was next to her, running an impersonal eye over her body. "You weren't hit?"

Her teeth were chattering and she couldn't seem to stop them. "They barely had time to get a shot off. And they didn't have that many archers to begin with."

"Didn't want to damage the merchandise." He sat down next to her and watched the captain load the ballista with an enormous bolt wrapped in a pitch-laden rag. Old Pert set the rag on fire and *THWAAAANG*, Laogonus launched the ballista for the fourth time. It hit the pirates amidships. He followed it with two more fire bolts.

One of the torches ignited the sail. It went up with a whoosh and soon the mast and rigging were alight and crackling. The heat from the fire could be felt from the deck of the *Thalassa* even as the two ships drifted farther apart.

More of the pirates jumped overboard. One of them made it as far as the *Thalassa*. Leon shot him in the throat when he was halfway up the side. He fell back into the sea without a sound, the water closing over his face.

The cries from the pirate ship did not cease until it had followed him down into the blue depths of the Middle Sea.

"Cover your ears," Apollodorus said.

"No." She had helped sink a ship and kill its entire crew. She would not hide from the consequences.

The last cry ended on a gurgle and when Tetisheri stood on shaky legs she saw the top of the other ship's mast sink inexorably beneath the sea. A wide, circular ripple spread out from the sinking and disappeared as Leon and Bolgios and Pert picked off the last survivors. The bodies ceased thrashing and floated, motionless, among a quantity of lines and deck boards and boxes and sacks from the ship.

Birds began to gather, and after them, the sharks.

Laogonus and the crew collected the bows and remaining arrows and stowed them below, along with the two unspent projectiles, which Tetisheri was glad to see they handled very, very carefully. The tarp once again covered the ballista and was securely lashed into place, reducing it to an innocent, rarely used piece of ship's tackle.

As Ra set in the west the wind came up again, strongly, out of the north-northwest. "A gift from Pontus," Laogonus said.

"If a belated one."

He looked down at Tetisheri, who had come to stand by him at the tiller. Above their heads the stars winked once again into existence, and a promising glow in the east presaged Sefkhet's rise. "You did well today. You've trained."

She hesitated. It wasn't really information he needed to

know, that she and the queen both had been tutored in self-defense by the Five Soldiers at Auletes' own command. "Yes," she said. "Uncle Neb insisted I know how to defend myself if I were going to be traveling with him."

"You learned well. An extra bow is always welcome."

She was silent for a moment. "You aren't just the queen's private courier." It wasn't a question.

The sail luffed and he leaned on the tiller, bringing the bow a bit to port. The sail bellied out again and the *Thalassa* leaned a little harder to starboard. Their wake was a comforting boil astern.

"I come from a family of sailors," he said. "My father, my uncle, my older brothers. We owned a small galley. We shipped anything anywhere east of Rome that would fit in our hold for whoever had the price.

"They were taken by pirates off Carthage. I was a boy still, home with my mother in Alexandria. They just—vanished. My mother— Well. Let's say she died of sorrow and leave it at that. I was taken on by a fisherman who knew of my father. He wasn't kind but at least I ate. I worked for him until I was of an age to go out on my own. Eventually, I became the captain of the ship I was working on.

"And then, fourteen years after they vanished, my uncle returned. As everyone had assumed, when our ship was taken they'd all been sold as galley slaves. The ship he was serving on was attacked, appropriately, by pirates, and in the confusion he managed to free himself and escaped into the water to swim to shore. He found a billet and worked his way back to Alexandria. His wife had died, his children didn't know him. Sobek's balls, I didn't know him. But at least he died at home, not at the oar."

He adjusted the tiller a fraction. The *Thalassa* responded to his hand like a lover leaning into a caress. "I'd always taken every opportunity to sink pirates wherever and whenever I found them. Sometimes, Poseidon's favor being what it is, I had to run. I hated those times. I wanted to do more, to kill more pirates. After my uncle came home, I wanted that even more. I'd come across this model of a ship on a trip to Punt, and I thought it might suit my purposes in the Middle Sea. I will say she caused a bit of a stir as I was building her at Dorian's Boat Yard. I suppose that was how I came to the queen's attention. At any rate she sent for me, heard me out, and offered to finance the *Thalassa* if I would run it as her private courier."

"How did you convince her to trust her cargoes to a ship without oarsmen?"

She heard the smile in his voice. "Pirates are a plague to shipping on the Middle Sea and Alexandria is its biggest port. It serves her interests to support my hobby. Becalmed, without oarsmen, the *Thalassa* looks like a juicy target." He patted the tiller. "They don't know she's bait for the trap until they swoop in and she shows her teeth. And then—" She felt him shrug.

"What about those poor wretches at the oars?" She could have said that his father or his brothers might have numbered among them, but didn't.

"They're better off at the bottom of the sea," he said. "Even they would say so."

"And you, your crew, the danger to you all—"

His voice was hard. "We know the risk. We have sworn an oath to each other that none of us will be taken alive."

She shivered.

"Are you cold?" Apollodorus had come silently up behind them.

"No," she said. "What was that powder in the first shot?"

Laogonus chuckled. "My dear Tetisheri," he said, "ask your friend. She designed it. She designed and built them all. She is very well read in the classics."

"None better," Apollodorus said.

After a while Tetisheri left them to curl up in the bow and try to get some sleep. She was not successful, not even when Apollodorus lay beside her and covered them both with his cloak. When the light of Pharos winked at them out of the darkness the next morning she had never been so glad to see it.

But as the dawn lightened the sky they were forced to wait to enter the harbor, because Julius Caesar, after nearly a year in Egypt, after fighting and nearly losing and finally winning a war, after defeating one ruler and impregnating another, this of all days was the day Caesar had chosen to depart.

"He can't even stay long enough to see his child born," Tetisheri said.

"I would imagine he has received some pretty stiff

messages from Rome," Apollodorus said. "Pharnaces seems a true son of Mithridates, in that he isn't happy unless he's invading his neighbors to geld their men and enslave their women. Rome has to be terrified that they're going to see a repeat of Mithridates' massacre. I don't think the Roman population in Anatolia has recovered its numbers even yet."

Laogonus put the *Thalassa* in the lee of Pharos and dropped anchor among all the other delayed vessels, and the entire crew lined the port rail to enjoy the spectacle.

Spectacle it was, ship after ship with oars keeping time to the drum, so many of them beating as one that it was as if the earth's heart was beating in time with them. Trumpets blared, singly and together, many painfully out of tune but no less enthusiastically for that. Fat-bellied supply ships, pontos and corbitas riding low beneath the weight of Egyptian grain and treasure, made their ponderous way north. A flurry of pennants snapped from every mast.

Warships took pride of place, from the lighter trireme built in the Greek style to the massive Roman liburnica and the smaller triconters with their three sails. Some of the warships were large enough to bear the mass of ballistas and catapults twice the size of *Thalassa*'s, all of them out in the open, displaying Rome's military might for all to see and be intimidated by.

Ra lit the armor of the soldiers so brilliantly one could not look directly at it. "That must be the whole of the Veteran Sixth Legion," Apollodorus said.

"What's left of it," Tetisheri said.

"He's been recruiting. And doubtless there are more legions waiting on him in Pontus."

Alexandrians lined the walls and shore of the city, cheering and waving, and the trumpets responded with even more fervor. "She's marched them all out today," Apollodorus said. "Including herself."

Tetisheri followed his eyes to the tiny platform above the mirror at the very top of the lighthouse. There stood a slender figure dressed in white and gold, the bulge of her belly prominent even from here. The Double Crown shone every bit as brightly as the Roman armor, and the crook and flail were crossed on her breast.

An especially loud and inharmonious blare of trumpets drew their eyes back to the mouth of the harbor, where emerged a liburnica bearing red sails. Caesar himself, in full legionnaire lorica from helmet to greaves, stood in the prow next to the aquila of the Sixth.

"I'm just a common soldier, me," Apollodorus said, "I wear the armor of the Senate and People of Rome just like every other Roman soldier I send out against the enemy. The troops must love that."

"Why he does it," Laogonus said.

Tetisheri clutched Apollodorus' wrist. "Look!"

He followed her gaze. Cassius Longinus stood a few steps from Caesar, like him dressed in full lorica. His helmet cast a shadow over his eyes but Tetisheri had the feeling he was looking straight at her.

A few steps behind him stood Polykarpus, with Petronius and Naevius at his side.

"Apollodorus!"

"I see. There is nothing we can do, Tetisheri." His voice fell and she barely heard what he said next. "There was nothing we could ever do."

Caesar saluted the queen, who bowed in return, and the population of Alexandria went mad with joy, or gave their very best imitation of it, under the eyes of their queen as they were. Caesar's ship was out of earshot before the tumult died.

And that joy was of course conditional. Alexandrians could be joyful that they had such a powerful ally so closely connected to them. They could also be joyful to be seeing the back of him.

Whatever they were feeling, they felt it loudly. "My ears are ringing," Laogonus said, working the tip of his finger into one and wriggling it.

She turned to Apollodorus. "What shall we do?"

To Laogonus Apollodorus said, "We'll dock in the royal harbor." To Tetisheri he said, "She saw us. She'll expect a report immediately."

Charmion met them at the side door and brought them to the same little balcony where they had foregathered, what was it now, only nine days ago? Food and drink had been set out on the small table and Cleopatra sat in one of the three chairs. She'd changed from her regalia into one of the simple linen shifts she preferred to wear when she was in private.

She greeted them with a smile. "Tetisheri. Apollodorus. Sit. Forgive me for not serving you. My son—" she patted her belly "—is taking exception to every move I make today. I think he's unhappy that his father is leaving us behind. Yes, I'll take some juice, thank you. No, nothing to eat. There's no room left for food." She accepted the cup and sipped at it.

For a few moments there was silence. The rising sun filled in the shadows left behind by the night, bringing the vast cityscape of Alexandria into sharper focus, twinkling off the ripples raised by a gentle breeze in the harbor below. Boats large and small slipped in and out of port to the crying of gulls and the profanity of dockmen and sailors. Tetisheri drank it in and felt refreshed and rejuvenated. Alexandria never failed her.

"Well. And what did you discover while you were away?"

Apollodorus looked at Tetisheri and raised his cup. Over to her. She took a drink, sorting her thoughts into a narrative that would explain most if not all of the events of the last two weeks. "I can't prove everything that I suspect," she said. "In fact I have very little proof at all of any of what I believe happened. Witnesses are either dead or gone or can't be found. The physical evidence is scanty at best."

"You're not in court here, Tetisheri. There are no scribes present to take down what you say and put it into the record. There are only the three of us. Speak, and leave nothing out. It is your job to report. Leave the conclusions—and the judgements—to me."

Tetisheri bowed her head. "As you wish, my queen." She took a deep breath and let it out slowly.

"Ptolemy hates you and wants you dead, and if he can manage it at the same time, he wants Arsinoë as his co-ruler instead. He knows, none better, that the only reason he's on the throne beside you is that Caesar needs the appearance of continuing tradition to keep the Alexandrians and Egyptians quiescent, and, not coincidentally, convince the Senate in Rome that he hasn't turned Egypt into his own personal fief. The fact that he owes his place on the throne only to Caesar's political necessity chafes Ptolemy unbearably, as does the fact that Caesar clearly favors you. So long as Ptolemy lives he will listen to and aid in any plan that subverts you and shortens your reign.

"Such a plan came his way, I believe, by Polykarpus. Polykarpus was Arsinoë's closest advisor. I believe he still is and that they are still in contact even though she is imprisoned in Rome. I believe she sent him here to do what he could to destabilize your reign.

"Ptolemy, as your co-ruler, has access to the workings of the realm. He knew of the order of the new coins, and told Polykarpus. Polykarpus, in turn, cast about for co-conspirators, and the less intelligent and inexperienced the better."

"Why?" Apollodorus said.

"The less intelligent his partners, the better able Polykarpus is to lead them by their noses," Cleopatra said.

"Exactly," Tetisheri said. "And so we come to Hunefer, who is—was—deep in debt with no means to repay it, and his Roman friends, Naevius and Petronius, young, reckless, no judgement, I would guess also in desperate need of money as young men seem always to be. A lot like Ptolemy Theos, in fact. Naevius and Petronius, not coincidentally, also happen to be closely related to the queen's agent in Cyprus, the man best placed to bring this theft off successfully."

"Paulinos was ever a reliable agent," Cleopatra said sadly. "I never had cause to doubt his probity or his loyalty until now."

"He lost his wife last year," Tetisheri said. "And sent his daughter off to Rome to live with his cousin Cassius' family."

Cleopatra said nothing, but her eyes betrayed her. Nothing would ever be adequate to excuse a thief, not when they were stealing from her.

Tetisheri sipped her juice. "From Polykarpus' viewpoint— and Ptolemy's—if they get away with the robbery they have struck a successful blow against your reign, while enriching themselves considerably into the bargain."

"And if they don't—" Apollodorus said.

"And if they don't," Tetisheri said. "Say, if perhaps Cassius learns of the theft."

"How?" the queen said.

"Khemit," Tetisheri said simply. "I haven't yet worked out how her suspicions turned toward Hunefer, but she questioned the Hunefer servants. Some one of them must have told Hunefer, who panicked and went to Khemit to threaten her to stay away from his house. Cassius was there and overheard." She turned to Apollodorus. "Remember?

Tarset said there was a Roman there that day, placing a large order."

"Would Cassius be shopping for his own linens?" Apollodorus said, raising an eyebrow.

"If it were a gift for his wife and daughters, perhaps," Tetisheri said. "At any rate, Cassius learned enough from eavesdropping that he went home and confronted his sons. They would have confessed at once—I doubt they have a single working backbone between the two of them—and blamed everything on Polykarpus. Cassius summoned Polykarpus and told him to clean up the mess before anyone else learned of the conspiracy or he'd spill Polykarpus' guts on the floor right there. He wrote Paulinos' daughter's name on a scrap of papyrus and signed it with his initial and sent Polykarpus to Lemesos.

"Paulinos saw this as the threat it most certainly was. His daughter was all that was left to him, and he probably counted on Cassius' family parading her in front of every eligible young suitor in Rome. He climbed into the bath and slit his wrist, I would guess with Polykarpus supervising, as this is not a man who leaves much to chance, especially not with an angry and powerful Roman breathing fire down his neck. Polykarpus burned the paper with Paulina's name on it, and in a rare mistake left enough of it behind to allow us to fill in the rest of the story." Tetisheri opened her satchel and produced the little bottle. "We have yet to determine if this is Cassius' handwriting, but if we can find a sample or someone who knows it I suspect we will."

"Cotta would know," the queen said. She pulled the stopper and shook out the scrap of papyrus, unrolling it carefully. After a moment she let it curl back up and replaced it in the little pot.

"Cotta," Tetisheri said, and then paused.

"What?" the queen said.

"Let me finish the story of the robbery and the murders first," Tetisheri said. "Polykarpus returned to Alexandria where Cassius greeted him with the news that Khemit was asking questions far too close to home. Make it go away, he said, and Polykarpus killed her with a blow from a sally stick."

Apollodorus said, "A sally stick is—"

"I know what it is," the queen said. "Continue."

"Frightened by Khemit's actions, terrified at the prospect of who else Hunefer had talked to, feeling like everything was unraveling, either Cassius or Polykarpus or both of them together decided they should make a clean sweep of it. The new issue was moved from its hiding place—I would bet somewhere in Ptolemy's quarters, because he is just that smart—to Hunefer's house. After which Hunefer was killed on his own doorstep by Polykarpus using the same sally stick that he used to kill Khemit. Thus insuring the discovery of the coins and shutting Hunefer's mouth once and for all.

"And then," she said levelly, "he joined Cassius and his sons at Uncle Neb's reception. I remember he came in late." Her laugh was entirely lacking in humor. "And we were the perfect alibi, were we not? A known friend to the queen?

A business operating under a Royal Charter signed by your own hand? Who could suspect anyone under that roof?"

They sat in silence as Ra climbed higher into the sky, the noise of a city at work increased, and the shadows shortened around them.

At length Cleopatra stirred. She peered into her cup and held it out. "He's finally asleep and I'd as soon not wake him up."

Apollodorus rose to fill her cup. She sipped, looking out over the Royal Harbor at Pharos and beyond. "No trouble with pirates on your journey there and back again?"

Apollodorus and Tetisheri exchanged a glance. "Only one, majesty. We were becalmed for an afternoon during our return."

The queen took this with very little change of expression. "What happened?"

"We sank her," Apollodorus said. "The luck was with us."

The queen smiled. "It usually is, with Laogonus."

Easy for her to say, Tetisheri thought. Another time she might take issue with her friend for sending her into danger unforewarned, but at the moment she was just too tired. Her arms ached, too, from the unaccustomed bow work. She wanted some of Keren's salve and a long, uninterrupted sleep in her own bed. She only hoped when she closed her eyes she would not watch the men they had killed die over and over again in her dreams.

The queen drank some of her juice. "While you were gone I had Ipwet put to the test."

Much of what Tetisheri had suffered beneath the roof of the House of Hunefer had come at Ipwet's hands, but she felt a chill nonetheless. "Did you?"

"Yes." Cleopatra met Tetisheri's eyes. She looked tranquil, which given the topic under discussion had to be an effect of the pregnancy. Tetisheri remembered the last weeks leading up to birth only too well—the feeling of overwhelming lethargy, the omnipresent urge to urinate, the swollen ankles, the lower back pain, the constant need for sleep warring with the complete inability to find a comfortable position in which to seek it out. Of course, Cleopatra had wanted her baby and might even have enjoyed its conception, which might make these last days somewhat easier, even if the father of her child had abandoned both of them for the charms of putting down a rebellion in Pontus.

"And?" Apollodorus said.

"And while she claimed not to be an active co-conspirator, she knew enough to confirm much of your conclusions."

"'Claimed?'" Tetisheri said.

"Alas." Cleopatra studied her cup, as if calculating whether the baby had left enough room for that last mouthful of pomegranate juice. She decided it had and drank, the strong muscles in her throat working. "Ipwet did not survive her test." She put the cup down and met Tetisheri's eyes again. Her own were perfectly serene.

Tetisheri had been sold into virtual slavery by a mother hungry for status. Cleopatra had seen it happen and been powerless to stop it then. She had bided her time until she had enough power to exact an overdue but she would consider just vengeance. That Ipwet's confession aided an ongoing investigation into theft and treason, Cleopatra Philopater, Seventh of Her Name, would see as only a bonus.

Apollodorus broke the silence before it became so heavy it crushed them all. "I can't say that she will be missed." He examined a stuffed date before popping it into his mouth. "What happens to Hunefer's possessions?"

"Sold at auction to satisfy his debts." The queen smiled. "I've already contacted Nebenteru to conduct the auction. I thought perhaps his fee might go toward the support of the slave girl you, ah, liberated from Hunefer the evening my dear brother had the effrontery to kidnap you."

"It's always a comfort to a woman to have a little money laid by," Tetisheri said with an effort. She took a deep breath and let it out as unobtrusively as possible. "Cassius left with Caesar. And Polykarpus with them, and Cassius' sons. We saw them all four on the deck of Caesar's liburnica."

The queen sighed. "Yes, I know. They appear to have escaped the queen's justice." There was a curious lack of rage in her matter-of-fact statement. "You were saying about Cotta."

"Cotta?" Tetisheri said. "Oh. Yes. He met us the morning before we left for Cyprus, after we had seen you. He seemed almost—giddy?—at the death of Hunefer and the recovery of the coin. He said that with the new issue returned and the guilty dead I could have nothing left to do but go back to my little import/export business. At which he was pleased to say that I seemed to be very successful." The queen raised an eyebrow. "He, too, attended Uncle Neb's reception the night before."

"Did he," the queen said thoughtfully. "Did he indeed."

"He knew something about the theft," Tetisheri said. "Perhaps not all, perhaps only in its later stages, but something. And he suspected that you had tasked me to investigate. It wasn't the first time he had sought me out."

"What?" said the queen.

"What?" said Apollodorus.

"You will remember, he was with Caesar when he came to you here, where the three of us first spoke of the theft. He must have had me followed because he called on me the next morning."

"He did what?" Apollodorus said. "You said nothing of this to me."

The queen kept to the subject at hand. "What did Cotta say?"

"Well," Tetisheri said, "the first thing he said to me was 'Not a cook, then.' I think he wanted me to know that he knew who I was, that there was nothing that happened in Alexandria of which he was unaware."

The queen laughed out loud.

Tetisheri smiled, albeit reluctantly. "Yes, I know. He complimented my Latin accent and hinted that perhaps I had learned to speak it when I accompanied you and Auletes to Rome."

"He was fishing," Apollodorus said.

"I believe he is watching you very closely, my queen,"

Tetisheri said. "And anyone you summon to the palace will also be watched."

"Let him watch." Cleopatra slid forward in her chair and accepted Apollodorus' hand in hoisting herself to her feet. "We have the new issue back. That is the most important thing. Thank you, Apollodorus." She smiled at Tetisheri. "Tetisheri, I can't thank you enough for your help in seeking out the truth in this matter."

"I didn't do much, my queen," Tetisheri said ruefully. "I was late to events everywhere I went."

"Nonsense," said the queen. "And now, my friends, I must leave you." She grimaced. "I have an interview with the nomarch of Wadjet. He was short on his tithe of grain. I sent to know why and he sent his wife to make his excuses."

"How long ago?"

The queen seemed to ponder. "How long ago was that, now? I think it was Pharmouthi. Toward the end of Peret, at any rate."

Tetisheri and Apollodorus both laughed. A ghost of a smile crossed the queen's face. "He has come to retrieve her, or so I believe. If he hasn't the conversation will go in an entirely different direction. And she is young and very lovely." She kissed Tetisheri lightly on the cheek. "I will see you soon, Sheri. Thank you again, so much, for your help."

"One last thing, majesty." Tetisheri produced the Eye of Isis from her purse, and Cleopatra received it into her hands.

"You did the Eye proud, Tetisheri. I know Khemit would agree."

12

The Fourth Week of Choiach
at Thirteenth Hour on the Second Day...

Shemu passed into Ahket. Hapi was kind and the Nile flooded on schedule, fertilizing its banks with the rich black silt that was responsible for feeding so many on the shores of the Middle Sea, and for the permanence of the throne beneath the behinds of three hundred years' worth of Ptolemies and four thousand years of Pharaohs.

A week after their return, Apollodorus finally tracked down Ineni's farm and brought Tetisheri there. The new bride was already pregnant and radiant with happiness, although she was grieved to hear of Khemit's death. She remembered Hunefer's sandals, and her description of the wealthy Roman's long face and lugubrious expression could have belonged to no one but Gauis Cassius Longinus. But she was able to add nothing to what Tetisheri had not already known, and Cassius was in Rome and far out of the queen's reach.

And so the favor Cleopatra had asked for Tetisheri was complete. Atet and Ineni received Tetisheri's wedding gift of a deep blue glass fruit bowl with gratitude and promises to stay in touch, and Tetisheri and Apollodorus returned to the city.

On the third day of the third week of Thoth Cleopatra gave birth to a son, Ptolemy XV Philopater Philomater Caesar, known as Caesarion. Mother and child were both healthy and thriving. Reports that Ptolemy XIV Theos Philopater had died choking on his own rage at hearing the news proved, alas, untrue.

The celebration went on for a week, with lavish offerings made to every god, Greek and Egyptian and Roman, for the boy's health, happiness and long life, with each temple large and small vying with the others in ceremonial pomp. Even the Jews sent a delegation bearing rare and precious stuffs from the East to the Palace, and were given the thanks of the queen in person. But then the Jews had always felt an affinity for this Ptolemy, who had suffered her own exile and who had on her return to power made them welcome in her city, where Arsinoë had not.

Less formally, the Alexandrians grumbled and the Egyptians cheered. The former did so discreetly. The latter paraded in the streets from Alexandria to Syrene.

Aurelius Cotta presented the queen with a solid gold charger big enough for a baby's bath with the history of

Alexander the Great in bas-relief around the edge, accompanied by a tender message from Caesar. No one mentioned that the gold it was made from originated in Nubia and was very likely part of Cleopatra's tribute to Rome.

The festivities were further enhanced by the issue of the new drachma featuring the images of the royal mother and son, an action welcomed by anyone and everyone who conducted business in Alexandria. Tetisheri and Uncle Neb noticed an uptick in business almost immediately, with Egyptian bronze replacing Roman and Greek silver in transactions almost two to one.

One enterprising entrepreneur commissioned a tiny bust in the image of Cleopatra and Caesarion from the coin and mass produced it. It proved so popular it had given rise to a dozen different knockoffs, and a profitable time was had by all. At least until the queen's treasurer asked for her due, but by then the little bust of the queen and her son was the first thing anyone saw walking through any door in Alexandria, private or public.

In Hathyr news came of Caesar's victory over Pharnaces, and of Caesar's report of the battle to the Senate and People of Rome. "'Veni, vidi, vici?'" Apollodorus said. "It's amusing, certainly, but that use of the first person—'*I* came, *I* saw, *I* conquered'—must have annoyed the hell out of Cato and the rest of those dreamers still hoping for a return of the Republic."

"You think it unlikely?" Uncle Neb said, his pearl taking an inquiring tilt.

Uncle Neb had lately returned from a trip to Rome where he had delivered a hold full of white papyrus. It had proved so profitable that, inevitably, he decided the only thing to do when he returned was host a twenty-course dinner for family and friends. They were crowded in around the massive display table in the warehouse on benches and stools, as Uncle Neb disliked the Roman custom of eating reclined on a couch—"It's just an invitation to spill one's dinner down the front of one's tunic. I have better places to put my food. And my wine." Apollodorus and his four partners, Keren, a few of Uncle Neb's friends in the trade and their wives were in attendance. Tetisheri invited Laogonus, who brought his wife, Sadek, a statuesque woman from Philae who Tetisheri immediately liked.

Nike, still wearing her invisible crown, gave the impression that they were fortunate indeed to be waited upon by her. Phoebe outdid herself in the kitchen, aided by Nebet who even Phoebe admitted had a fine hand with savories. This was a favor on Nebet's part, as a loan from Tetisheri had funded a food cart on the Way near the Library—all those hungry students. By a special dispensation from Uncle Neb she'd managed to salvage most of her cooking pots from Hunefer's kitchen before the house mysteriously burned to the ground, most fortuitously after all its of contents had been sold and a tidy sum realized on Nike's behalf.

"Did she sow the ground with salt, too?" Apollodorus said when he heard, but then of all of them he had the fewest illusions when it came to their queen.

There was no loss of life, and nothing remained of the House of Hunefer but a few charred timbers. These were soon cleared away in preparation for the construction of a park and playing fields, a gift of the queen to the people of Alexandria and Egypt.

"A return of the Republic? Unlikely?" Apollodorus said now. "Indeed, I think it impossible." He was helping himself to seconds of the meltingly tender lamb braised in apricot sauce. "Caesar must have accumulated enough power and wealth by now, even for him."

Much of it right here in this city, Tetisheri thought.

"He's bound to spend it where it will do him the most good. The Romans, the ones not in the Senate, love him for all the treasure and slaves he has sent their way, and love even more all the lands he has acquired for the greater glory of Rome, a piece of which they are all hoping to acquire for themselves. Not to mention the Egyptian grain. The Romans love their bread and their blood. When he finally gets home they'll give him a triumph and replace the laurel with a crown, and he'll import the best Greek architects to build them a new amphitheater in Rome itself so gladiators can kill each other for their viewing pleasure."

Dub exchanged a look with Crixus and said smoothly, "Yes, but he won't have it all his own way, surely?" and the rest of the table plunged eagerly into the discussion while Apollodorus concentrated on his plate.

Tetisheri had not missed the acid note in his voice. It nursed a suspicion that had been forming since the queen's mission had first thrown them together, since Cotta's questions had piqued her interest and suggested a possible conclusion so outrageous she hardly dared name it in her own mind.

Tetisheri and Apollodorus had spent a great deal of time together over the last four months. They'd gone to the races at the Hippodrome, attended a production of *Lysistrata* in the original Greek at the Royal Theater, listened to a lecture on Herodotus from a visiting scholar specializing in geography. When he was not busy with some task for the queen or tending to the Five Soldiers, they spent time in walks all over the city and talked of everything but the events of Mesore past, and laughed a great deal. He improved on acquaintance, did Apollodorus. He was intelligent, he paid attention to what one said and remembered it, he seemed to actually listen when she spoke instead of giving the appearance of waiting until she stopped talking so he could start. This alone was a rare enough quality among men to render him memorable.

He had attempted nothing physical beyond kissing her. He seemed to be waiting for something. She didn't know what but she was beginning to grow impatient.

Uncle Neb sat at one end of the table, his face flushed and his pearl atilt with enjoyment, his friends and family gathered on either side, herself opposite him, all of them enjoying themselves every bit as much as he was, the wit and the wine flowing in equal measure. The Five Soldiers fitted in well, thoughtful, and well-spoken when they contributed to the conversation. Isidorus, his white hair in curls that stood up like little horns, contributing a rude jest but not so rude as to offend the ladies present, and the eldest easily by fifteen or twenty years. Dub, dark and swarthy, he looked like a native of Barcino, Castus and Crixus, the red-headed Alemanni, and Apollodorus, tall and fair.

Her heart thumped hard, once, in her breast and for a moment she forgot to breathe.

It would please me very much indeed to encounter the pirates of Brundisium.

She leaned over to Isidoros, who was sitting next to her. "Did you all come from Sicily?"

He blinked at her, confused. "What?"

"The five of you. Did you join the Roman Army in Sicily? Is that why they call Apollodorus the Sicilian? Because he isn't, is he? Sicilian. None of you are."

He narrowed his eyes. "Some things are better left unsaid, Tetisheri, and believe me when I tell you, that is one of them." He paused. "Are you—" He hesitated, and looked from her to Apollodorus and back again.

"I don't know," she said with a rueful smile.

He looked as if he were barely restraining himself from kicking Apollodorus under the table.

"—such a tragedy, both sons dead," Uncle Neb said, shaking his head.

"Cassius' sons, that was?" Crios said. Crios was a fellow trader and friendly rival. He left the travel to his partners while he stayed home to mind the business but he was always interested in the gossip from abroad. Gossip from Rome in particular was always valuable for trade. "They made something of a name for themselves while they were here, and not a good one. Wenching whether the wench was willing or not, drinking the tavernas dry, brawling in the streets—" He shook his head. "They gave the Shurta more to do in a shorter space of time than any dozen young nobles of Egyptian blood you could name. I always thought the king was foolish to befriend them but then, you can never tell Ptolemy anything." He tut-tutted. "Chilon says not to speak ill of the dead, but, really, those two young louts will surely not be missed by anyone except, possibly, their family."

Tetisheri sat up with a jerk, her conversation with Isidorus forgotten. "Cassius' sons are dead?"

Uncle Neb looked at her. "Yes, the two boys that were here with him when they were all here with Caesar. Naevius and—Pontius? Portius?"

"Petronius," Tetisheri said through numb lips.

Apollodorus stared at her across the table, his eyes very green, but he said nothing.

"How did they die, Uncle?" Tetisheri said, her voice sounding not quite like her own. "Did you hear?"

Uncle Neb grimaced. "They were carousing in some whorehouse down in the Subura and both ate from the same dish of bad mushrooms. As I heard the story others there that evening sickened as well, but only the two boys died."

Enough, and it heals.

Too much, and it kills.

Bast must have had her hand on Tetisheri that evening, because she managed to remain at the table for the rest of the meal, and even through the cheese and fruit that followed. She stood calmly next to Uncle Neb at the door, it seemed in someone else's body, to bid their guests a fond farewell.

Apollodorus had remained behind, as she had known he would.

"I'm going out for a little, Uncle," she told Neb. "I won't be too late, and Apollodorus will be with me."

"He will, eh?" Uncle Neb said, as he had said many times before over the past four months. "Well, well, I suppose if Apollodorus is with you—" He smiled benignly, although his eyes were sharp as they flicked back and forth between the two of them. Nothing was lost on Uncle Neb, and Tetisheri knew he was expecting some kind of declaration from the two of them. But he would never push. It was one of many reasons she loved him.

She'd left the house at a near run. About halfway to the palace she slowed to a walk. Apollodorus kept pace beside her, making no attempt to engage her in conversation. He hadn't asked where they were going, either. They had both naturally turned left as they stepped out the door.

Stars gleamed in the sky overhead, but there was no moon, it being that time every month when Sefkhet rested from her labors. The air of an Alexandrian summer evening brushed against the skin like the finest silk. The sounds of a city at peace filled the spaces in between the darkness. A baby cried and was silenced at its mother's breast, a woman moaned her pleasure in her lover's arms, a old man told a ribald tale. No one took any notice of the two of them until they reached the palace and were recognized. A short time later they were brought before the queen.

She received them in one of the smaller reception rooms this time, a much more formal venue with an actual throne, less ornate than the one in the Great Hall but a throne nevertheless, establishing a note of formality instead of friendship.

That suited Tetisheri. She wasn't feeling very friendly at the moment.

In dress, too, Cleopatra was every inch the queen. She wore the uraeus on her brow, a severe linen shift topped with a wide collar of carnelian and gold, and she held the crook in her right hand.

Better than the flail, Tetisheri thought.

Cleopatra looked alert and composed. If they had roused her from her bed she didn't show it.

Tetisheri bowed, taking her time, putting every ounce of grace into it she could muster, offering her sovereign her due. "Majesty."

"Tetisheri, we are pleased to see you again," the queen said. "You have heard the news, no doubt, that we are safely delivered of a son?"

"I have, majesty, and the news fills my heart with gladness, for you and for him, and for the future of Egypt." That much at least was true. "The infant thrives?"

"He does. I have sent word to his father. I am expecting a summons to Rome."

Tetisheri met Cleopatra's eyes without flinching. "That prospect must give you equal joy, majesty, of being reunited with your husband."

They stared at each other for a long moment.

Surprisingly, Cleopatra broke first. "Leave us," she said.

Apollodorus bowed and turned to go, as did the half dozen retainers and guards who had been stationed around the room. The click of the door closing behind them echoed faintly off the walls, bare but for the paint of frescoes illustrating the lives of Isis and Osiris and Horus, their son.

Cleopatra tossed the crook to one side and yanked the cobra from her head. She scrubbed her fingers over her scalp and sighed. "That's better."

The shadows of sleeplessness were gone from beneath her eyes and her waist had regained its original shape. In the absence of the trappings of royalty she looked much more like Sheri's old friend Pati. However, the throne was raised high enough so that anyone speaking to the sovereign would perforce be looking up. She remained seated, deliberately so, Tetisheri was certain. Cleopatra VII Philopater never did anything without a reason. As Tetisheri, who had known her longer and better than most, had cause to know she seldom did anything without two or three reasons. Thrifty, that was their queen.

"Well?" the queen said impatiently. "Your message said it was urgent."

"You turned Polykarpus," Tetisheri said.

The queen raised her eyebrows. "I beg your pardon?"

"I saw him." A chill slid over Tetisheri's flesh at the brief memory of a long-nosed man vanishing into the shadows of the palace. "The day you sent Apollodorus to bring me here. I didn't know who he was but I saw him, here, in your palace. Which means you turned him before you let him leave for Rome, before you let any of them leave for Rome. You couldn't let anyone who had anything to do with the theft of the new issue go unpunished, but you couldn't kill two sons of a Senator of Rome in Alexandria, not with Caesar in residence. Probably not ever, not without severe reprisals. Even Caesar wouldn't have been able to let you get away with that." She paused, struck by another thought.

"What?" the queen said.

"You turned him before that," Tetisheri said. She looked at her queen, her friend, and marveled at the unsuspected depths of her guile. "He's been your creature since... when?"

It wasn't really a question and Cleopatra didn't answer. Tetisheri took a slow turn about the room, pausing here and there to trace the features of Egyptian gods and all their wonderful, improbable regalia.

"Of course," she said, coming to a stop, and turned to face the queen again. "Of course. Since Arsinoë was captured and sent to Rome. You snapped him up before Ptolemy thought of it."

Cleopatra sat very still on her throne, her hands resting on its arms, her spine straight, her face without expression.

Attach a ceremonial beard and she would look just like the cartouche of Hatshepsut on that worthy's tomb in the Valley of the Kings. Another forward-thinking queen of Egypt, energetic, ambitious, a tremendous builder, a proponent of trade.

A woman determined to rule alone, against a tradition that had stood with very few exceptions for four thousand years.

"You sent him to Ptolemy's court, who naturally thought Polykarpus was his to command. Instead, Polykarpus spied on him and made his deepest secrets and conspiracies known to you. Which means..."

She walked back to stand before the throne, to stare up at her queen.

"You knew about the theft of the new issue from the moment the idea was broached in your brother's court."

"Know your enemy," the queen said. "As I believe we read together from some scroll in my Library."

"You sent him into Ptolemy's court to find out what he could," Tetisheri said, "as you now have sent him to Rome." She remembered him standing on the deck of Caesar's liburna, a pace away from Petronius and Naevius. "As tutor to Cassius' sons, perhaps? Ptolemy would think that such a position would be perfect for assimilating the news from Rome, and Cassius would want to keep Polykarpus close. And all the time he works for you." She shook her head. "I wonder how he manages to keep his allegiances straight."

There was a brief silence. When the queen spoke again, what she said was unexpected. "How did you guess?"

"Uncle Neb has just returned from Rome, where he heard that Cassius' sons were dead of poison. I knew, then." She quoted the queen's words back at her. "'Enough and it heals. Too much and it kills.'" Deliberately said, she thought, just as she had been deliberately received in Cleopatra's stillroom that first morning. "You sent Polykarpus to kill them, and you sent the poison with him." She thought of the poison bomb exploding on the pirates' deck, the choking, killing cloud enveloping the men there. "Poison you very probably made yourself."

The queen sighed. "Yes. Well. A thorough grounding in herbs and spices and their medicinal and culinary applications—and their tactical ones—is always useful. And one must never delegate something that crucial to others unless it is absolutely necessary." She met Tetisheri's eyes. "They stole from me. Did you think I would not punish them for that?"

Given what she knew of her queen and friend, there was no world in which Tetisheri could imagine Cleopatra doing so. "So," she said. "Your brother wishes to undermine your hold on power, perhaps even to bring back Arsinoë to reign at his side. You knew he would find Polykarpus's pedigree, that of Arsinoë's chief advisor, irresistible, especially when Polykarpus offered him a plan that would strike a blow at the very foundation of Alexandria and Egypt: its commerce. Alexandria and the Nile are essential to trade on the Middle Sea. If it has no coin of its own to spend, it becomes a debtor nation and a client state, most likely of Rome. We are already in debt to Rome because of your father's borrowing so much from Pompey to regain his throne."

"Not any more we're not."

"Oh, you've managed to pay that all back? What was it, again? Ten thousand talents? Or did Caesar just take it with him when he left?"

Cleopatra raised her chin. "The father of my child and the heir to the throne of Alexandria and Egypt may draw upon us as he chooses."

"Unless and until he strips the treasury and the granaries bare."

The queen's eyes flashed. "I know how to take care of my own."

"Better than Ptolemy Theos, certainly," Tetisheri said, refusing to be intimidated. "That, I grant you."

She took another turn around the room. "Why, then, this farce of an investigation?" She meditated on that for a few moments. "Cotta?" She looked at the queen. "I see. Cotta's main concern was that no Roman be found to be involved in the theft of the new issue, at least until they were out of your reach. And you could not be seen to know any more details of the theft than was good for you by Cotta, your watchdog."

"Better the conspiracy exposed and the guilty identified," the queen said. "Cotta did not, does not need to know that I knew that Hunefer was not alone in his guilt."

"What about Khemit? You tasked her with finding the coin, knowing it a fool's errand every bit as much as it was mine. You do remember Polykarpus, your own creature, is thrice a murderer? That he killed Khemit, Longinus and Hunefer? Are your citizens—is your own *Eye* of so little value to you that you may see their lives spent so cheaply in your service?"

Some expression too swiftly come and gone to identify crossed the queen's face.

"I see," Tetisheri said slowly. "By then Polykarpus had his instructions. He was to obey Cassius in all things, and when Khemit got too close to the truth Cassius told Ptolemy. And Ptolemy ordered Polykarpus to kill her." Her mouth twisted. "After all, he was only following your orders to at least appear to obey your brother in all things."

The silence lay heavily between them.

"You have done well, Tetisheri," Cleopatra said at last. "Far better than I had hoped."

Tetisheri raised an eyebrow. "Have you been waiting for me to hear of the boys' deaths?"

Cleopatra smiled. "I may have been curious to see if you would put it all together."

"Congratulations, my queen," Tetisheri said flatly. "You must be so pleased."

"Tetisheri—"

"There is one other matter that requires your attention, my queen." She could see the effort it took for Cleopatra not to roll her eyes but she knew what she had to say would be unwelcome and she was determined to keep the coming revelation in the most formal tone. "Are we entirely private here?"

The queen's eyes narrowed. "In this room, I'm as certain as I can be that we are."

Tetisheri bowed again and walked to the door. Opening it, she looked at Apollodorus, who had taken up his usual station outside. "Please come in, Apollodorus."

Apollodorus looked at her for a moment without expression, before shifting his gaze to Cleopatra. "Is this your wish, my queen?"

"Evidently," Cleopatra said, her eyes fixed on Tetisheri, her face a still, golden mask.

Apollodorus came inside and closed the door behind him. Tetisheri motioned him forward and the queen descended the steps to her throne so that the three of them created a tight, tense triangle. He was as calm and attentive as always. She forced herself to meet his eyes. "Apollodorus, you arrived in Alexandria with the Roman Army the year before Auletes was expelled from Egypt."

His voice was deep and firm. "I did."

"And here you left the army to open a gymnasium catering to young nobles, offering instruction in the arts of swordplay, the bow, the staff, wrestling, soldiery. Each of your four partners had a specialty in one or two of these arts."

"Yes."

"Although it is said that your skill with the trident and the net was first among all. We saw you work with it ourselves, when we were students there." She indicated the queen. "You were a wonder to behold. No one could defeat you, no matter what weapon they chose."

The silence in the room was absolute.

"The others were equally skilled, Dub as a murmillo, Is

with the bow, Crixus and Castus as boxers beyond equal. Is was older by a generation but like you he could still turn his hand to any weapon. Your business was so instantly success-ful that it brought you in a very short time to the attention of the king."

Apollodorus nodded once. His face was every bit as mask-like as the queen's, but he didn't move to stop her, and neither did Cleopatra.

"You say you are from Sicily. Apollodorus the Sicilian is how you are known to Alexandria."

"Yes."

"Cotta himself commented on how little you look like a Sicilian, that men of your size and coloring come most often from Thrace." She swallowed hard, and was relieved when her voice remained steady and assured. "As are you, yourself, I believe. Thracian. Not Sicilian at all." She gestured. "You wear the Thracian double-headed eagle on your gauntlets. There is a shield with a double-headed eagle on it that takes pride of place on the wall of your gymnasium. You told me you were born in the third year of the reign of Saladas I. There is no reason for you to be familiar with the reigns of Thracian kings or to know the years of the one you were born in, not if you are from Sicily."

He regarded her for a long moment, his expression as impassive as the queen's. "It would not be the first time a man came to Alexandria whose history began again with his first step on shore."

It was neither an acknowledgement or a denial. "No," she

said. "Alexandria was built by immigrants, beginning with Alexander himself. It wouldn't be the first time this week such a man might take on a new identity to begin a new life, never mind the year you arrived."

She glanced at the queen, who sat immobile and oddly incurious. She might be a spectator at a duel with no money on either contestant. "However, in this case I would draw your attention to the disappearance of another Thracian almost thirty years ago. A Thracian believed dead, killed by Crassus at the battle of Silarus. A slave, a former gladiator, one known as a retiarius. One who, so the story goes, had four generals, one, like him, from Thrace, two Alemanni, and one it was thought from Barcino. One whose revolt came nearer overthrowing Rome than any other attempt ever has. One whose name is to this day used by Roman mothers to frighten their children into obedience. One who—"

"Say not his name," the queen said. "Not even here."

Cleopatra's gaze held a distinct warning. "As you wish, majesty." Tetisheri bent her head and turned back to Apollodorus. "Isidoros is the most wonderful storyteller. When classes were over he kept us of all enthralled with tales of the gods on Olympus, and the Olympic games." She paused. "And of famous bouts in a ludus in the city of Capua, some forty leagues south of Rome on the Appian Way.

"He spoke of many of the gladiators there as if he had known them. Indeed, as if he had fought them. And with them." She looked down at her hands, fisted together so tightly that the bones seemed to show through her knuckles. "Once, in passing, he spoke of a particular lanista, one Gnaeus Lentulus." She shrugged. "Everyone knows who the most famous graduate of Lentulus' ludus was."

She sighed. "You're not him, of course, you are much too young. But his son? As your companions were sons of his generals? As Isidorus was, perhaps, one of his younger soldiers? That any member of that revolt survived and is alive and living in Alexandria would be anathema to the Romans. That his own blood survived would be intolerable. They would kill you all outright, did they know."

There was a little silence.

"That will be all, Apollodorus." There might have been some emphasis on the name. Cleopatra smiled at him. "Thank you."

"My queen."

Tetisheri waited until the door had closed behind him, just. "You knew," she said. "You knew!"

The queen permitted herself a small smile.

"Since when?"

Cleopatra ignored the lack of honorific in the demand. "My father knew immediately, although Apollodorus will not repeat that conversation, not even to me. Father told me when he named me heir."

"But not your brother."

"No." Cleopatra's lip curled. "Not any of my siblings."

Auletes believing, perhaps, Tetisheri thought, that any one of them would have sold Apollodorus to Rome the moment their father breathed his last. And not without cause. She thought of Arsinoë and Ptolemy, willing even to sell out their country to Rome so long as that sale brought their sister down with it. "Was this some kind of test? Some... some exercise to prove my intelligence, my ability, my loyalty?" And then, fiercely, she said, "Did you tell him to sleep with me?"

It might have been the first time Tetisheri had seen Cleopatra look surprised since she took the throne. But then her eyebrows twitched together and there was no mistaking the anger that edged her voice. "No, Tetisheri. No, I did not." She paused, her lips tight, as if trying repress what else she wanted to say. If that was the case, in a moment of rare candor she spoke her thought. "Because I have no choice in bed partners does not mean I think no one else should have free choice, either."

Tetisheri wasn't sure she believed her.

"Who else knows?" the queen said.

She wasn't asking about Tetisheri and Apollodorus. "Cotta knows that Apollodorus is not what he appears, but he has no proof and he's aware that Apollodorus stands high in your favor. He will make no public accusation. Or he won't until such an accusation serves Caesar's best interests."

"Surely you mean Rome's best interests," the queen said dryly. "Who else?"

"Aristander may suspect, but he is your loyal servant and he wouldn't admit such a thing even to himself. Sosigenes knows everything else so he probably knows this, too, although he has never said so, or even hinted at it. Other than Castus, Crixus, Dubnorix, and Isidoros, no one else."

Without moving the queen seemed to relax, ever so slightly. "Aristander has ever stood my friend, and Sosigenes." The queen smiled. "As have you, Sheri."

Since the only response was a polite bow, Tetisheri bowed politely.

"I owe you much," Cleopatra said. "What can I do to demonstrate my gratitude?"

Tetisheri gave a short, humorless laugh. "Other than killing Hunefer and Ipwet and destroying any trace of their previous existence on this earth?"

The queen chose to answer obliquely. "The enemies of my friends are my enemies as well."

And only recently had Cleopatra obtained the power to demonstrate that fact, which would explain why she had had to wait until now to exact what Tetisheri suspected would become a very Cleopatrian kind of justice on those enemies.

The queen was still waiting for an answer. "Well," Tetisheri said finally. "I'd like to kill your brother. If that could be arranged."

Cleopatra snorted. "Yes, well, so would I. If that could be arranged."

"Failing that, I'd like to be there when he is killed."

"No, Tetisheri," the queen said, almost sadly. "No, you would not."

Their eyes met, and Tetisheri remembered the dying pirates

and their ship being pulled inexorably into the fatal embrace of the Middle Sea. "No," she said after a long moment. "No, I probably wouldn't."

Alexandria and Egypt had been co-ruled by brothers and sisters for its entire three hundred years, and for four thousand years before that by the pharaohs, and Caesar had insisted it continue thus in at least an outward show of respect to Alexandrian and Egyptian norms. And so it would continue. For now.

They smiled at each other. Cleopatra's smile faded first. "I have asked much of you these past months, Tetisheri. None knows how much more than I. Now, I must ask even more of you."

"Majesty—"

The queen turned and climbed the steps back to her throne. She reset the royal cobra on her brow and picked up the crook to assume the formal pose of ruler of the Two Kingdoms. "Caesar has crushed all of Europe beneath Rome's heel, and they need our grain and they want our gold. Here at home, the Alexandrians despise the Egyptians and me for trying to place the Egyptians on an equal footing with themselves. But if I don't, the Egyptians will not hesitate to rise up against me if they see no opportunities to achieve some kind parity with the rest of the citizens of Alexandria.

"I walk a tightrope, Tetisheri. If I fall, Ptolemy will ascend the throne, and he will ask for Arsinoë's return from Rome to rule with him. Caesar will grant his wish because above all Caesar needs Alexandria and Egypt at peace and productive of tithes. The two of them will be totally subservient to Rome. Better Rome than making common cause with their own subjects. And Alexandria and Egypt as we know it will cease to exist."

She raised her chin. "But I, Tetisheri, I am not only the queen of the citizens of Alexandria, but of all of the citizens of Upper and Lower Egypt. If Alexandria is the heart of the country I rule, then Egypt is its soul. I walk a tightrope, yes, and I need your help to keep my balance."

Cleopatra held out her hand, the Eye of Isis in all its lapis and nacre glory cradled in her palm, the mother of pearl gleaming in the light of the candles.

Now Tetisheri understood the reason for the room in which Cleopatra had received her this evening. She could feel the weight of the badge of office from where she stood. A burden she had anticipated from the morning she had first seen it, on the little balcony overlooking the Royal Harbor. "Please, Pati," she said, her voice barely above a whisper, echoing the same words she had said to her queen on that morning. "Please don't ask this of me."

"Who else can I ask, Sheri?" the queen said, gently but inexorably, echoing her own words in reply. "In all my realm, who else can I trust to be my eyes, my ears, my voice?"

It was a smooth, flat circle of polished lapis, one side plain, the other inlaid with a luminous circle of mother of pearl smaller than the base, itself inlaid with a smaller circle of turquoise that was more green than blue by contrast with the lapis. The piece was exquisitely made, the inlays so carefully crafted and applied that they appeared part of the lapis itself, so that all three layers of gemstones appeared as one. It was the only one of its kind, feared as soon as it was known, respected as much as it was feared. The Eye of Isis, the eye, and mouth, and hand of the ruler of Alexandria and Egypt.

Once more Cleopatra descended from her throne, meeting Tetisheri on level ground, and raised the Eye in both hands by its chain.

It settled so precisely between Tetisheri's breasts that it seemed to have been made to lie there.

The queen smiled, and bowed low in recognition and honor to the new Eye of Isis.

EPÍLOGOS

The door closed behind her.

"Did you accept?" he said.

She began to walk and he fell into step beside her.

"Sheri," he said. "Did you accept?"

She gave a swift look around to make sure there was no one else nearby. Realizing what she was doing, realizing she was already adopting the caution and the care of the spy, she made an exclamation of annoyance and reached into her bodice. The Eye gleamed in the light of the lamps of the palace as if it were alive, awake, aware, observant, seeing all, forgetting nothing.

He sighed. "Good."

She replaced the Eye in her bodice and walked on. "You, naturally, would think so."

"I beg your pardon?"

She walked faster. "Wasn't that your job, to seduce me into accepting this one?"

He halted momentarily as she boiled up the hallway, making for the door. She almost made it.

A firm hand grasped her arm and insisted she stop. "Sheri. Tetisheri. Look at me."

She fixed her gaze on the dark green of his tunic.

He sighed again and put a hand beneath her chin, raising her face until their eyes met, hers angry and uncertain, his steady and unflinching. "How did you know?"

She shrugged. "It wasn't that difficult."

"*Skatos*, I hope not," he said.

She couldn't help smiling at his dismay. "And that was how I knew for sure."

"What is how you knew what?"

"You swear in Greek." He looked taken aback, and she elaborated. "Had you really been Sicilian, you would swear in Sicilian. A Roman soldier, retired, in Latin. And these." She tapped his wrist guards. "The two-headed eagle is the symbol of Thrace. And—"

He watched the rich color flood into her face. "And?"

She glanced away. "You make love in Greek, too," she said, her voice barely above a whisper. *Agape mou.*

He kissed the tip of her nose and led her by the hand back into the warm, dark evening. The stars above seemed somehow brighter than they had been before. They began to walk slowly eastward.

"Isidorus told us the story, which was much the same for all our fathers. He was eleven and large for his age," he said. "The Romans came, conscripting for their army. They would have killed his family did he not join. And then one of their officers saw him in the training yard. He had some aptitude at arms. He decided my father would show to advantage in the arena and sold him to Lentulus." His lips tightened.

"So young?" She slid her hand into his. It closed convulsively around hers. In the distance waves lapped at the shore. "How was he defeated?"

He sighed. "There were so many of them, from so many different places. Everyone had their own idea of how and when to fight. You can't fight a war that way. Well." He shook his head. "As Isidorus says, you can't fight a war that way and win."

"There were rumors that he meant to escape, that he had hired the pirates of Brundisium."

He nodded. "But they betrayed him. It's what killed them all in the end. All except we five."

"How did you escape?"

"Isidorus was fifteen and my father's aide. On the eve of the battle of Silarus, he put us into Is's care and sent the five of us to Rhegium, where we boarded a ship for Sicily."

"Bast above. A fifteen-year-old boy and four babies. I would like to have seen that."

He laughed. "To hear Isidorus tell it he would rather have died at my father's side. He settled us in Syrakousai, hired a wet nurse and a maid and found work as an instructor at a small ludus nearby."

"No one suspected?"

"If they did, they valued Isidorus too highly to inform on him. He is very good, you know."

"I know."

"We grew up on the sands of the arena there. I don't even remember the first time I held a gladius in my hand. When we were old enough, we joined the Roman Army. Eventually, we found ourselves here." He was silent for a moment. "It was said to be a good place to start over. A place where it didn't matter who you were or where you came from, it only mattered if you had something of value to contribute. Isidorus bought us out and we founded the Five Soldiers. Auletes—" He sighed. "Well, Auletes was never a strong man, but he was far from a stupid one. He came to the gymnasium and watched us work. The court followed him, as courts do." He laughed a little. "You could say he brought us into fashion. A little while later, he summoned me to the Palace." He shrugged. "The rest you know."

"You have not lived an uneventful life, Apollodorus."

He laughed again, but this time it was free of bitterness. "In spite of my profession, in spite of the work I do for the queen, my time in Alexandria has been the most peaceful of my existence." He looked at her. "It seems possible I may have a life as other men have lives. Marriage, perhaps. Even children."

She swallowed hard and looked away from those penetrating green eyes. "I have had no success at either."

He slid an arm around her waist and pressed a gentle kiss to her forehead. "I won't rush you, Tetisheri. But it is only fair that you know what I want."

"It is almost too much," she said. "The theft. The murders. The Eye." She sighed. "You. It is a great deal to take in all at once. I thought I was born to be a trader, that I would remain one all my life."

"You still are a trader, Tetisheri. It's just that now you are something more. As Khemit was something more." He looked down at her. "Our queen chose well when she chose you."

She looked away, still unwilling to accept or believe it herself. "Was this, us, was this truly not part of her plan?"

He caught both her hands in his and forced her to meet his eyes. His own were serious and intent. "I have wanted you for so long I can't remember a time when I didn't. When Auletes first blackmailed me into becoming his daughter's personal guard you were both only twelve and at that time I felt a hundred. As you grew up, I seemed to—I don't know." He looked away, considering. "Not grow younger, obviously, but at least grow into life again. To think that perhaps I wasn't too old for you after all." He looked back at her and smiled, a little grimly. "And then, just when it seemed to me that you were looking back at me the same way I was looking at you, your mother married you off to Hunefer."

By unspoken mutual consent they turned and began to walk again.

"Did you—"

"No," he said firmly. "No, Tetisheri, I did not kill your mother." He looked up at the night sky. "I admit I would have liked to, especially when she sold you to that *kólos*. But there is already enough blood on my hands without admitting to more that I did not spill."

"Do you know who did?"

He was silent for a moment. "Do you really want to know?"

She sighed. "No. No, I suppose not."

He held her hand in his, warm and hard. "So," he said, "do you have plans for tomorrow evening?"

"I beg your pardon?"

"Remember the taverna that Renni the Egyptian is starting in front of the Five Soldiers? He opens tomorrow. The first glass of athiri is free—"

"I thought he wasn't serving alcohol."

She heard the smile in his voice. "We're making an exception this one time. He is making enough dolmas to feed the entire Sixth Legion, if it were not off laying waste to Pontus. All of Alexandria has been invited."

She found she could bear to look at him again, after all. If the night hid every wrinkle and scar, the close-cropped fair hair, the broad brow, the deep-set green eyes, the firm-lipped, smiling mouth, the determined chin, still she could see them in her mind's eye, so very dear for so very long. She wondered what he saw when he looked at her, but whatever it was must have been pleasing enough to him for him to smile at her in just that way.

"Well," she said. "One has to eat."

ACKNOWLEDGMENTS

As always, my thanks to Michael Catoggio for his swift responses to my cries for research help.